HIDE ISLAND

HIDE ISLAND

RICHARD BURGIN

Texas Review Press
Huntsville, Texas

FIRST EDITION, 2013
Requests for permission to reproduce material from this work should be
sent to:

Permissions
Texas Review Press
English Department
Sam Houston State University
Huntsville, TX 77341-2146

Acknowledgement:

For their generous help and support I'd like to thank Chris Cefalu,
Edmund de Chasca, Doreen Harrison, Paul Ruffin, and Jessica Rogen.

Cover Art: Steven Kenny, "The Arrival", 2012, oil on canvas 72x 60 inches

Library of Congress Cataloging-in-Publication Data

Burgin, Richard.
    [Works. Selections]
    Hide island : a novella and ten stories / Richard Burgin.
        pages ; cm.
    ISBN 978-1-937875-67-1 (cloth; alk, paper)
    ISBN 978-1-937875-22-0 (pbk. : alk. paper)
    I. Burgin, Richard. Atlantis. II. Title.
    PS3552.U717H53 2013
    813'.54--dc23
                            2013013291

For my beloved son Ricky

CONTENTS

HIDE ISLAND

ATLANTIS

She sat up in bed, rigid but strangely alert, as if trying to identify the sound of something underwater. When he touched her shoulder to try to make her lie down again she turned toward the wall.

"What's wrong?" he said.

She shook her head back and forth.

"Rina, come on, what is it? You're scaring me."

"I don't feel good."

"Take a hit of that joint on the bureau. It'll help."

"How long we gonna go on like this, huh? What's your plan, Stacy? Is there one?"

"What do you mean? I don't understand."

"Course you don't understand," she said, finally facing him. "Things going along pretty much the way you want? Just stay high every minute with me under the ground in this tomb that's below sea-level, for Christ's sake."

"I'm not high every minute." He wanted to

add that his place wasn't below sea level either, but he wasn't 100% sure if it was or not.

"C'mon, can you face reality just a little? You wake up and have a Quaalude so you can take a shower then to counteract that you smoke a joint so you can have sex with me in the morning. Then to get through the day you take more Quaaludes or sometimes E. Then it's back to Xanax so we can watch TV and go to sleep. What do you think, you're gonna die if you aren't high for a minute?"

"I thought you liked being high with me."

"Yeah I do. Everyone likes being high but not every minute of every day."

"Okay. We'll cut back a little. I'll cut back."

"It's not just the drugs."

"What?"

"We never go anywhere. We never do anything."

"This is Fort Lee. You think we're really missing something? Besides, we go out sometimes."

"Sure. We make heroic little runs for food to the deli or sometimes we even make it to the supermarket. We have to get high to do that, too."

"We've gone out at night."

"Just so you can get more drugs or more money to buy drugs. How come we never go to New York anymore?"

He felt a surge of anger but told himself to stay cool.

"I thought we agreed we'd had enough of New York," he said, turning his head away, hoping to see a bit of a tree, but the venetian blinds were closed.

"I meant living there, I'd had enough. I didn't mean never visiting. I'm sick of these wannabe dealers and crack whores you see here all the time."

"It was one guy and his girlfriend. You're exaggerating."

"I'm sick of all the other Fort Lee zombies, too. I'm too young to live like this, to just give up."

He was scared now. Something in her tone of voice and in her eyes frightened him. "I didn't think we were giving up," he said softly.

"What did you think we were doing?"

"I thought it was more like taking a little break, like a kind of vacation."

"This ain't a vacation. We're just dying is what it is."

"Come on, you don't mean that. You're exaggerating again."

"I do mean it. We have to get high to go to the bathroom and nobody's washed a dish in a week."

He felt himself start to vibrate then. He didn't know if it was from the pot, his Viagra, or if it were somehow cold in his apartment though it was close to the end of June.

"Okay, you tell me what you want me to do?"

"Jesus Christ!" she said, looking at the little clock on the bed table. "It's almost three in the afternoon. My sleep patterns are completely destroyed." She put her hands over her eyes as if she were going to cry but then got out of bed decisively. "I know what I'm going to do. I'm going to take a shower and then I'm going to get some food for us, and while I'm gone, you think about what we're gonna do."

"You worried about money? Is that it?"

"I'm more worried about what you do to get your money. Okay? We're setting ourselves up to get in a lot of trouble one day. Your landlady gave me a funny look yesterday."

"A funny look? Big deal."

"A killer look that said 'Bitch, I'd just as soon off you as not.' I feel like any day she could call the cops."

"She won't do anything. She wants her

money, too. Who else would take her bottom floor and pay what I do?"

"You sure about that? I think it's time to go some place else for a while is what I think. But you think about it while I'm out. You focus on it without getting high first if you can and when I come back you tell me what you came up with, okay?"

She had to know how he'd feel, didn't she? Hadn't he jumped out of bed right after she said it and volunteered to go shopping with her? But she insisted she wanted to go alone so he could think, in other words, worry. That was Rina in a nutshell—Runaway Rina he'd nicknamed her in his mind a long time ago—who'd run away from home as a teenager, and never came back, first from Vineland to Atlantic City, then from San Francisco and finally from New York with him to Fort Lee. Come to think of it, his own mother would sometimes leave or threaten to leave him and his father, too, whenever she wanted to get back at them for some perceived deficiency or slight, of which the world had no end, of course, so why take the lackings of the world out on your family? The vibrating was getting worse, and he was feeling more and more cold. He pulled the blankets up on his shoulders and tried to get warm.

He thought of something else then. A woman who looked like Rina could do anything and might well be doing it right now with anybody. He pictured her breasts—smallish but with oversized nipples, when they erected. He'd never seen nipples like that before and knew he never would again. They were once in a lifetime nipples—he was only 31 but already knew that. The first time he saw them erect he'd nearly come just from looking at them. How could she have done him the way she did just a few hours ago and then gotten angry enough that she'd left him like this? There was no logic with Rina, ever, so he could never relax with her. The slightest thing could upset her and then he'd worry that she'd leave him or else screw someone else, which amounted to the same thing.

He got out of bed and took a Quaalude from the bureau. What would his father have done in this situation? He'd been with his own Rina all those years. Of course it was absurd to compare himself to his father who was so much more mature and honest than him and who barely even drank, much less took any drugs. His father was emotionally strong all right, in a way he never could be. He'd stayed over forty years with Stacy's mother—a woman he should have left but didn't. What hadn't he endured? The death of his parents, his brothers and sisters. Career frustration, raising two difficult children, especially him. But never drank, never really complained, even after his stroke from which he finally passed. He always tried to help everyone, especially his hypochondriacal wife. Never cheated either and even quit smoking on his own at the age of 62.

His father was physically strong, too. Once during one of their family vacations in Atlantic City when he was only seven or eight, he went in the ocean holding his father's hand because the waves were big, enormous to his child's eye and stronger than any water he'd ever felt. It was a little scary because he couldn't really swim much then, and when the waves came they'd crash over his head and knock him down. But his father never stopped holding his hand. He could feel his hand under water as if it were stronger than the surf, then feel and see it again when he emerged from underwater. He remembered laughing, squealing with delight, and his father laughing too, only letting go of his hand when they reached the sand in front of the Boardwalk.

How exciting yet strangely innocent the Boardwalk was then! Little kids ran freely up and down it laughing and yelling and carrying their cotton candy like magic wands. There was a fun house then, around where the Taj Mahal was now, and horses still dove into the ocean from the old steel pier. One time his family went to the Miss America pageant, and he picked the winner, young as he was, Miss Ohio, which made his mother marvel at him. Still, what he remembered most was jumping the waves with his father, holding his hand firmly as they crashed over him.

But this was becoming too painful to remember. What was the point of getting things you loved if you could never get them back again, if you could only lose them, as if life was nothing but an extended game of Hide and Seek? And now Rina was playing another form of Hide and Seek with him.

He decided not to wait for the Quaalude to hit and began smoking the joint he'd left for her on the bureau. It was the right decision, he said to himself, as he finally lay back under the blankets.

...When she walked in carrying the groceries into the tiny kitchen he was still lying down pretending not to be high. She began putting the food away quickly and didn't answer him when he said hello.

"So did you do some thinking?" she finally said, coming into the room at last.

"Yeah, I did."

She stood in front of him, dressed in her tight blue jeans, staring at him, waiting.

"How'd you like to go to Atlantic City?" he said.

*   *   *

They were driving at least five miles under the speed limit so they wouldn't risk being stopped (not trusting the landlady, they'd decided to bring their whole stash with them) when he sensed something, a kind of tense quiet that permeated the closed-in space of the car. For a minute he debated whether to ask her what it was—always a dangerous question these days. If only she'd followed his advice and had taken a hit before they left or at least taken a Xanax, but she was stubborn that way. She was trying to set an example. He turned on a rock radio station he thought she'd like (he would have preferred jazz or classical), but her mood didn't change. That was her method when she wanted to talk about something—to just disappear into a cone of silence until he couldn't take it anymore.

"You're being pretty quiet," he said, deciding to play it halfway.

"I'm just wondering about things."

"What things?"

"I'm wondering why Atlantic City? Why exactly are we going there?"

"I thought you liked to go swimming, you always did before."

"I do like swimming, but there are plenty of other places we could go on the shore where we could swim."

"It's the same ocean, isn't it? And Atlantic City has the Boardwalk."

"So you think we have the money to stay in a hotel there?"

"I told you not to worry about money, baby. We can afford to stay there for at least a   few nights."

"And I guess you don't plan to do much gambling then?"

"Not if you don't want me to," he said, silently congratulating himself, not only on his answer but that he thought he really meant it. "So have I answered all your questions?"

"Some of them."

"Only some of them?"

"I have issues with Atlantic City, too, you know."

Then he remembered that she used to work as a dancer there before they met in New York. He'd never asked her too much about that. Atlantic City was also where she went first when she ran away, so he could understand her mixed feelings.

"So what do you want? You want to forget all about it and just turn around?"

"I just don't see why we can't go to a quieter place to swim and cool out and be together. Some place like Ventnor or Margate or Longport, that's less tempting."

"What do you mean 'tempting'? What would you be tempted to do?" he said, thinking of her dance routine again.

"I'm not tempted to do anything there. I was thinking of you."

"Me? Why me?"

"I don't know. I can't help thinking you're planning a meeting with some big-shot dealer there. I think you'll be tempted to make some kind of score."

He felt his heart beat but kept his cool. Could she somehow know about Ike? Ike had really seemed to care about him, especially after his father died, gave him some prime territory to deal in. A few months ago, in fact, he remembered hearing that Ike had moved to Ventnor for a little peace and quiet. This was too good to be true, yet it was true. He could visit him in Ventnor, and Rina couldn't possibly object to that. He wouldn't have to set foot in Atlantic City except to visit the beach where he'd swam with his father. He could meet Ike in a clean, family-oriented place where he could even bring Rina.

"Okay, we can stay at Ventnor," he said. "That's cool."

She took his hand, which in itself made it all worth it. "Thanks, sweetie," she said, smiling.

"I like you, Stacy, you're a good kid. Whenever you're in Atlantic City you look me up, and I'll take care of you. You look me up and I'll set you up, deal?"

That's what Ike said to him the last time he saw him, a few years ago in Harrah's. There was always work from Ike and good money, too. Sometimes he even gave him a girl, and he'd get a free blowjob as a tip. Ike was a first class guy all around. He only dealt with the best people: first-rate dealers, hookers, and clients—all top of the line. Even when he'd moved to New York and started getting out of the business a little Ike still kept in touch.

"Tough without your old man, huh?" he'd once said to him, putting his arm around him in the Taj Mahal. "Wish my kid loved me the way you love him….You know, Stacy, maybe you should stay out of the business for awhile. Go back to college. That's what your old man wanted. He told me that more than once."

"Really?"

"Sure, you were always on his mind. He even told me once while we were playing bridge. Your old man was one hell of a bridge player, too."

"Did you ever tell him…?"

"About the work we do? Course not. You think I'm crazy? Your old man never suspected a thing. He was as innocent and pure as a child.

I loved the guy like a brother. You let me set you up with something big—a one-time deal I'll give to you instead of to my own son and then you go back and get your degree. Then we'll see about your future."

Sure enough in less than a month he'd set him up with a killer deal. "I offered a deal like this to my son, Dominic, but he thinks he's such a big shot in Vegas now that he don't need this no more," he said in a voice as bitter as he'd ever heard from Ike. "Believe me, he'll live to regret it all."

So he took the deal although he never finished college.

He was remembering all this while Rina was sleeping next to him in the motel room in Ventnor. He wouldn't postpone seeing Ike any longer. It was simply a question of explaining it to Rina. He was sure she'd be reasonable about it.

When he finally brought it up, they'd just come back from a swim, walking to their room with arms around each other's waists, hands sometimes tapping each other's bottoms. The ocean always had that kind of effect on him and on her, too. Once in the room they had sex quickly—not even bothering to smoke first. He felt hot and happy, and it seemed a good time to tell her, except that he was straight but he told her anyway.

"So let me understand this," she said, "we're here for what, three hours, we just finished making love, and you want to go out right now and see this old guy, who was a friend of your father?"

"I told you about Ike, he was like a father to me after my old man died. You even met him once or twice."

"I wouldn't say he was like a father to you.

More like the Godfather. He set you up big-time in the business is what you mean, and now you want to work for him again. Isn't that what this is about? I should have known that's why you wanted to go to A.C."

"You're way off, Rina, that's not it at all."

"Oh, so you wanted to come here to make me happy, making me come back to where I was at the lowest point in my life. You can't even bear to hear what happened to me in A.C., can you? Not even to this day."

He turned away from her and looked at a sliver of the sky barely visible through the blinds. How could a sky be both blank and blue, but it was. He hated it when she was sarcastic and bitter. "You can tell me," he said, hoping she wouldn't. "Really, you can tell me."

"Forget it," she said in her tough girl voice, though when he turned back to look at her again her eyes were moist. "I'm not making that mistake again. I don't need to tell you any of that shit 'cause I know it hurts you."

"Well I didn't bring you here to hurt you, either. You seemed like you wanted to come more than you didn't. And I wasn't even thinking about Ike when I suggested it, I swear. About your past, I guess I just blocked it out. I'm sorry."

"What were you really thinking about wanting to go to Atlantic City?" (She said the name of the place as if it were Afghanistan or North Korea.).

"Well number one it's an obvious place to go to for fun, not for you maybe, I understand, but in general, and second, I was thinking of my father and my family. We went to A.C. a lot when I was a kid. Those were good times for me, that's all."

He thought briefly of telling her how his father used to hold his hand in the water but decided not to.

"So you never thought of Ike at all?"

"I thought of him later. When you said you'd rather go to Ventnor or some place like it, I remembered then that he lived there now."

"And that's when you decided you had to see him?"

"Yeah it grew on me. I miss him, that's all. It's not about dealing."

"So why's he like you so much?"

"I don't know. He has problems with his own son. His son's about the only person in the business who had trouble working with him."

"But you said you were getting out of it. You said you were gonna get a real job or else finish school or both. You've said a lot of things to me."

"Said it and meant it. Look, why don't you come with me to see him? See for yourself. It's just about friendship, that's all. But friendship's a lot."

"No, I'm not gonna rain on your parade."

"Are you kidding? I want you to come. I'm proud of you. I wanna show you off, okay? I want you to get to know Ike. He doesn't need me to push his merchandise. Believe me, the guy has a fleet of workers and behind them a fleet of wannabe workers."

"Oh geez, I'm so impressed. It's almost like meeting Einstein, I guess."

"Come on, you don't have to be sarcastic. I'm sure you'll like him. And I really want you to come with me. I mean it."

She looked at him with a serious expression in her hazel-green eyes. It was strange. He had almost the same color eyes as her, but he knew her eyes expressed many more emotions than his.

"I must have to have my head examined to stick with you."

"What?"

"What? You're a drug dealer. You're gonna

get busted. Just like every dealer I've ever known. And you're gonna get me busted too."

"What are you talking about?"

"I must love to have tragedies happen to me. They got a word for people like me?" she said, getting out of bed.

He stared at her body in awe. Couldn't believe sometimes that she was his lover and knew then that he wanted her as his wife one day. But he couldn't tell her yet. Maybe later on when they'd finally go to Atlantic City.

"So what have you decided?" he said.

"I'm coming with you, you know that. But I gotta get ready first."

One other thing he loved about Rina, she always looked great when they went out. Not just good but appropriate for the occasion, too. It took her a lot of time, but it was worth it. This time it wasn't so bad because he hadn't smoked, which would make the time seem longer but had taken a 'lude he had in his pocket just to take the edge off waiting. Somehow Quaaludes and Atlantic City went together like a sunset over the ocean, he thought.

While she was primping, mostly with her hair and make-up, he found Ike's address in his old address book. He wondered if he should call him first but decided it would be more fun to surprise him. Then he wondered what he'd say if Ike wanted him to do a deal. Could he really say no to Ike? But anyway, that could wait for later. He knew Ike wouldn't ask him in front of Rina, especially with her dressed kind of conservatively in a light pink dress and her brand-new beach shoes that she bought back in Fort Lee. She was a classy woman, and Ike appreciated class. He was lucky, unimaginably lucky, to have Rina as his girl, he knew that. So what if she'd had to dance naked for a while years ago? The woman had been handed a nightmare life right from the start, her own father doing her when she was only 12.

"How do I look?" she said emerging from the bathroom with a big smile.

"Like heaven," he said.

"Now you're the one who's not talking," she said to him in the car. They were less than a mile from Ike's house, and he was thinking how nice her perfume smelled and how nice it would be to smell her when they made love later and then, for a moment, wondering why he was visiting a criminal, like Ike, however benevolent his personality might be.

"You feeling nervous about seeing him?"

He shrugged. "A little."

"Go ahead, have a hit. I'll have one too. It won't kill us."

"You mean that?"

"Yeah, of course. I ain't a cop. Pull over into that alleyway by the Italian restaurant. We can do it there."

They took their emergency traveling joint from the glove compartment, lit up and each took two hits.

"It's hard to stop, isn't it?" he said, "When the pot's so good."

"We can do the rest later after we see Ike," she said, suddenly looking sad.

"What's the matter, baby?" he said.

She said, "You know, it really isn't easy for me even being near Atlantic City. You know why I went there in the first place, don't you? I told you about my father."

"Yeah, of course you told me."

"I mean, why'd he have to fuck me, huh? What

kind of guy does that to his own daughter when I wasn't even 13 yet? He was already getting plenty of women on the side, you know, what'd he need me for?"

"Try not to go down that road, okay?" he said. "The pot will only make it worse."

"I just feel nervous lately, anxious, like something very bad's gonna happen. Do you understand? Like I'm gonna die soon or something. Do you know what I mean? Maybe it's just because we're so close to A.C."

He knew exactly what she meant. Lately, a lot of the time when he was straight, he felt that he was going to die soon too, a feeling only the right drugs could take away, but he didn't want to tell her that.

"Kind of," he said.

"I wish we were back in bed in Fort Lee doing it together. That's what I wish."

"We can drive back right after we see Ike. I'd like that, too."

"Really?"

"Yeah, really," he said, although he still wanted to see the beach, if only for a few minutes, where he once swam with his father. Maybe he could go there alone for ten minutes while she stayed in the car or else while she was in the motel in Ventnor packing (if they really were going to leave right away) though he wished somehow they could go there together.

"I like that all the time," he added to reassure her, "being in bed with you. Even in my grave I'll want it with you."

"Really?"

"No question about it."

"So you're not thinking of ditching me here and taking up with some loose bitch you meet in a casino?"

"No way, 'course not. It's just you I want, always."

"That's not the pot talking, is it? You don't just love me when you're on drugs, do you?"

"'Course not. I love you all the time," he said. "So, you feeling better now?"

"Yeah," Rina said, taking his hand and squeezing it.

"We're only a few blocks from Ike's. I think we should go see him now, okay?"

"Sure," she said. "I'm ready."

He noticed the tight, smallish white beach houses of Ventnor were suddenly sparkling. He felt blissed out. He looked at her and felt she was feeling the same thing.

"What are you feeling?" he said to her when they were two houses from Ike's. There was a strong breeze blowing in from the sea and it moved her hair in an attractive way.

"Like my problems are a million miles away."

He gave her hand another squeeze. "Me too," he said.

Then they started to walk up the steps to Ike's house, the largest one on the block where a number of low to mid-level Mafia reputedly owned homes.

He rang the bell, hoping he wasn't too stoned, but still glad that he'd smoked. He waited, then rang a second and third time. It probably took Ike longer to get around now that he was in his early seventies. He continued to wait until he felt a pair of eyes staring at him through the peep hold. An unfamiliar voice said, "Who is it?"

He felt then that he'd made a mistake and should excuse himself and leave. Instead, he said, "I came to see Ike. It's Stacy."

A few seconds later the door opened. The man who let them in was huge, both taller than him by three or four inches and heavier by fifty to seventy pounds. He was wearing a loose T-shirt that said "Hell Busters" on it, loose light-blue, low-slung jeans, black boots and lots of tattoos on his arms and neck, making Stacy think he might be Ike's bodyguard.

"Hey," Stacy said. "This is Rina."

Rina nodded and said a soft hello. There was something birdlike and sad in the little sound she produced.

"I'm Dom," he said, without extending his hand. "Wanna beer?"

"Sure," Stacy said.

"You too?" Dom said.

"Yes, thanks," Rina said, a little nervously.

Dom left the room and came back with the drinks, walking in a herky-jerky halting kind of way. Neither Stacy nor Rina felt they could risk looking at each other so both stared straight ahead.

"Sit down," Dom said, pointing to the generic-looking couch in the living room. "Take a load off." They sat down on the couch, Dom on a straight back chair facing them. While they made small talk about the weather, Stacy strained to see something that would remind him of Ike but couldn't. The furniture was much cheaper and more ordinary than Ike's would be. Ike was a man who liked nice things.

"Want another?" Dom said.

"No thanks," they said in unison. Stacy couldn't help staring at Dom's tough, inscrutable face—a collage of scars, wrinkles and stubble. He was definitely on some drug but Stacy couldn't tell which. "So is Ike around?" he said.

"No," Dom said. "He's not."

"Is he gonna be back soon?"

"No, not likely. Ike's gone forever, wherever forever is."

"That's too bad. I'm an old friend of his and I just thought I'd drop by."

"Yeah, I know who you are," Dom said, in a voice both matter of fact and sullen.

Stacy looked harder at him, but there was a blurred haphazard quality to Dom's face, as if it had run away from itself.

"You don't remember me, do you?" Dom said.

"I feel embarrassed but I can't say..."

"I'm Ike's son, remember now?"

"Sure, he talked about you a lot."

"I'll bet he did. Ike's not here though. I run things now."

"Oh, I didn't come about business."

"Really? You sure about that? I remember you were very interested in business. I remember you muscling me out of a number of deals. Yeah, you wanted to get my territory in Atlantic City and goddamn it if my old man didn't give it to you."

"That was so long ago."

"Was it? I remember it real well, and I ain't even gone to college like you did."

Stacy shrugged reflexively. "Well I'm not in the business now."

"Really? I think you're still trying to give me the business is what I think," Dom said, putting down his empty beer can with emphasis, next to the three other empty cans on the little white Formica table beside him. Stacy stared hard at him then as if to see him more clearly as Dom slowly withdrew a gun that his T-shirt had previously hidden. "I was wondering when I'd see you again, college boy. I was thinking of visiting you, but I couldn't find you. You must have been working on something big you wanted to keep secret from me and Ike but now, presto chango, you've come right to me."

Seeing the gun, Rina let out a little gasp.

"Shut up," Dom said, softly but

authoritatively, moving his eyes snake like for a moment in her direction.

"What's going on?" Stacy said.

"What's going on is what your late, great friend Mr. Ike would call a 'superior opportunity.' For me anyway," he said laughing. "See, I can speak fancy, too."

"I don't understand why you're upset."

"Upset?" Dom said looking around the room incredulously as if an audience were there he was appealing to. "Upset? You think I'm 'upset'?"

"Your father likes me. I'm a friend of his. We never had a problem."

"Oh, I know he liked you, matter of fact he fuckin' loved you. I told him you weren't worth a shit in the ground but he didn't believe me. But it don't matter what he thought anymore, does it?"

"What do you mean?"

"Weren't you listening, bright boy? Old Ike is dead. He's worm food now so it don't matter what he said or thought. I run things now. I run all his things: the business, this house, this gun," he said, waving it in the air briefly like a pennant.

"What happened to Ike?" Stacy blurted.

Dom looked down at the floor for a second. "Cancer," he said. "You heard of that, ain't you?"

"My father died of cancer, too," Stacy said.

Dom nodded curtly. "That so. You think that makes us brothers or something?"

He realized then that Dom was definitely on some kind of powerful drug. He didn't know what it was, only that it was strong.

"So I can see you're upset but..."

"Upset?" he said in the same incredulous voice, as he looked around the room again. "I ain't upset. Just 'cause I took out my piece to show you? I'm just having fun. If you knew me you'd understand. But you never bothered to know me. Bet you wish you had now. "Hey you," he said, pointing the gun at Rina, "show me your tits. I feel like seein' something pretty."

She looked at Stacy uncertainly for a second, but he said nothing, felt his face was frozen as if he'd had some kind of neurological attack.

"Come on," Dom said, pointing the gun at her. "I wanna see 'em now."

She took her dress off in a few seconds. She was wearing a black bra he'd bought her from Victoria's Secret.

"Take your top off, too. What're you, deaf?"

She took her bra off. Maybe someone would walk by and stop it, Stacy thought, a cop or someone from the neighborhood. Even if the neighborhood really was all Mafia they liked order and quiet, didn't they, and wouldn't want any unnecessary trouble or attention, certainly not a loose cannon like Dom, who could never fit in with them. Never.

"You know how to dance?" Dom said to her.

She looked at Stacy again, and he nodded to show it was okay with him.

"I can't," she said.

"You can't?" Dom said in that same incredulous voice that filled the room like a kind of nightmare organ. 'Course you can. Every girl knows how to dance. I'm sure you know how to dance, yeah. I've heard about you. Fact is, I'm pretty sure I've seen you, too. Yeah, I've seen all the dancers. 'Summer wave' I think your name was. I could have sworn that was your name in Atlantic City."

"That's not my name."

"It's not your name now, but it was once."

"No, it wasn't ever my name."

"I think it was. I've got a good memory for tits, especially unusual ones. Yeah, I remember your nipples, honey, remember 'em well. So, do me a dance."

She shook her head back and forth then looked at Stacy. "I can't."

"What's the problem? Is it Bozo over there?" he said, pointing the gun briefly in Stacy's direction. "I can get rid of him in a second."

"No, no, it's not him."

"Hey Bozo, tell the little lady to dance for me, okay? Tell her now."

"Leave her alone," he said, more weakly than he wanted to sound.

"Hey," Dom said, moving toward him and punching him hard in the stomach. "You don't tell me what to do, ever."

"Okay," Rina said, beginning to dance. "I'm doing it."

"See, I told you that you could. Now bring it a little closer to me."

Stacy was slumped over the chair.

She looked at him hesitantly, not knowing what to do, just like a little girl, he thought, as if the shock of the situation had drained her of her years.

"Don't look at Bozo to see what to do," Dom said. "Bozo's a clown, a sad, little clown who don't know what to do. You bring your tits to me, now!" he said, pointing the gun at her instead of him. She started to cry then.

Stacy tried to sit up in the chair. There was a sharp pain in his ribs. He must have been hit more than once because his stomach hurt, too.

Dom was hooting now like a cowboy at a rodeo as Rina continued to dance for him while she cried. Angel Dust, Stacy thought, Dom must be on some kind of Angel Dust or maybe meth.

She looked at him one more time, while Dom was unzipping his pants. "Hey, no looking at Bozo. I already told you that. Bozo don't have what you need, bitch. He's just got a little clown dick that don't give nothin' to no grown-up woman like you. You get on your knees now and open your mouth. I'm about to fill you up like you ain't ever been filled before," Dom said, laughing as he grabbed her head and holding it, firmly put himself inside her.

Stacy stared in disbelief for a few seconds, then got up from his chair and, lowering his head, charged at him, but Dom was surprisingly agile, moving his head like a matador and then hitting Stacy on the head with his gun two times. Stacy fell to the floor. He landed but felt like he was still falling, like a pebble that would keep falling in the depths of the ocean. Then he no longer saw anything.

When he woke up she was driving. She told him they'd left Dom's house almost two hours ago, that Dom was worried he'd killed him. Then she told him that she'd stopped at the motel and thrown their things in the car as fast as she could. "If you want me to, I'll take you to a hospital."

"No," he said, noticing that she was staring straight ahead (had barely looked at him even once). She was also talking in an even, expressionless voice like a zombie. Then he wondered if Dom had finished in her mouth, but knew he could never ask her. Hated himself for even thinking about it. He felt a pain in his head and ribs though it wasn't as bad as he'd remembered.

"I gave you a lot of Ibuprofen," she said, as if reading his mind.

"Thanks," he said.

She didn't answer.

. . . It grew quiet in the car, as if quiet could grow like a spreading plant. It got so quiet he felt as if they were in some other kind of machine seated far apart, like in a Ferris wheel, perhaps, somehow equipped to travel on the road.

No one wanted to hear the radio—they agreed on that—without even talking about it. Nor did they speak about possibly stopping for food. He felt sorry that she had to be straight now, but she was afraid to drive a long distance on any kind of drug, and she wouldn't let him drive, saying he was too beat up to do it.

After an hour or so, his thoughts about Dom faded a bit, and he began thinking about Atlantic City and how he'd never gotten to go to the beach where he had swam with his father, though that was the reason why he'd wanted to go there in the first place. It was funny, Atlantic City wasn't what you would call one of the beautiful places in the country like the Grand Canyon or Niagara Falls. It was probably beautiful once, of course, but that had all ended with the boardwalk and all the casinos. It was as if that once beautiful Atlantic City had sunk and was now like Atlantis, the lost island he'd read about as a kid.

Rina began crying but softly, as if they were tears shed during a dream. "I'm not going home with you," she said. "I'm going to drop you off and then stay with my sister in Brooklyn."

"Don't do that, please."

"No, I am," she said, with tears running down her cheeks now. "You'll be all right...I mean you can't want to sleep next to me tonight, or ever, so what's the point of pretending?"

"What are you talking about?"

"I'm trash, Stacy, I must be. That's why trashy things keep happening to me, don't you get it? That's why you take drugs all the time, 'cause you're depressed about being with me."

"Hey, stop it. Stop talking like that, okay? That's crazy talk. You think I blame you for what happened? If there's any blame, I blame myself for bringing you with me when I went to see Ike. You're innocent Rina, totally innocent. I shouldn't have gone to see Ike. I really just wanted to see where my father took me swimming."

"Why didn't you then?" she blurted.

"I don't know. I should have. Look, pull over, get on the soft shoulder, will you?"

"Why?"

"Just do it, okay?"

When she'd finally parked he took one of her hands in his. "I want us to forget about what happened," he said. "It was horrible but it's over and none of it was your fault."

"Are you high?"

"I'm not, no, no I'm not," he said, still holding her hand.

She didn't say anything. He could hear the cars whizzing by them in the dark, their headlights flying by like little bonfires.

"Are you losing it? Are you all right?"

He had been shaking but he wasn't now. He decided he would never ask her about what happened with Dom.

"I'm not losing it," he said. "But if you talk about leaving me, I will lose it. So don't ever say it."

She looked at him and nodded. "Yeah, okay, I'll try to believe you."

"Good, that's good," he said looking down at the floor for a moment. When he looked up he saw a single car pass by with only one headlight.

"Stacy, let's go back to your place. That's what I really want to do," she said, adding, "I'm sorry I called it a tomb."

"It is a tomb, but it's our tomb, isn't it?"

"Yeah," she said. "It's our tomb."

THE REUNION

In the last six months or so I've noticed that my handwriting, even my signature, has gotten smaller, almost as if I'm trying to withdraw whatever it is I'm saying before I've said anything at all. Immediately I attributed it to my age (although I have no proof it's age related), to just another way my body has started to betray me.

Nobody teaches you about getting older. There isn't a course that prepares you for it in any school that I know of. You hear jokes about it all the time; you see an occasional image of an old person flicker across your TV screen, but those figures are inevitably in ads trying to deny or postpone age. Whenever "seniors" (that euphemistic title society confers upon the old as if they've finally earned a highly desired promotion) are on TV, they're smiling as they play tennis or paint houses or embrace their grandchildren. But really, beginning in your sixties, most people are alone as, one by one, they begin to lose control of their powers.

For my 63rd birthday, I decided to visit Brookline, a suburb just outside of Boston where I spent my childhood. I'd been having recurring dreams about the house I grew up in, dreams that shook me to my core. They must have been powerful for me to overcome my anxiety about travel (flying in particular)—something else that's increased these last few years.

I went to a hotel near Copley Square in the heart of Boston and took a longish walk to the public gardens. One thing about Boston that I especially like is that so many parts of it remain unchanged, which, of course, makes it easier to remember, and these days my memory needs all the help it can get. Copley Square, for example, with its old churches and public library and the gardens with their formal flower arrangements and swan boats, is much the same as when I first saw it as a child.

I took another walk the next afternoon up and down Newbury Street, which had changed somewhat, at least from the way I remembered it. The first part of the street was filled with the most expensive stores in Boston, like Armani and Gucci. The second half had one outdoor European-style café after another. The women, sometimes scantily clad, were heartbreakingly beautiful as they sat composed at their tables or else paraded down the street themselves. Were they that alluring when I lived in Boston many years ago or was this just another case of an aging man finding youth itself to be beautiful?

In any case, I soon began reviewing the romances of my twenties and thirties until that got too intense, and I began to get hungry. I left Newbury Street and found a Mediterranean restaurant on Boylston Street called Vlaro. The restaurant was literally underground, unusual for an upscale Boston eatery, and featured a bar and the largest flat-screen TV I'd ever seen that took up nearly half a wall. I was seated at the back part of the restaurant, partially protected from the television by a door of beads and a series of strategically placed plants. When I looked up, I realized I was facing an attractive brunette about 15 years younger than me who was, like me, alone.

Was this a gift, or trick of the hostess, or more likely a dumb coincidence? At any rate, I quickly realized it didn't matter because nothing would happen, since I no longer would try for anything in a situation like this. Still I couldn't help looking at her more than I should have. She had dark pretty eyes and appealingly thick lips. Probably she colored her hair, but if she did, she did an exquisite and quite convincing job.

I ordered a Greek salad and an Italian dish involving stuffed rice balls with tomato sauce. The food was outstanding, but I found myself looking at the brunette (wearing a compelling kind of purple frock) wondering if she were an Italian dish as well.

Then suddenly she smiled at me. (I told myself there was no one else in that part of the restaurant except the two of us so it must have been me.) Shortly after that she started talking to me. I was so surprised that I couldn't remember what she said at first, probably something like, "Is your food as good as mine?"

I told her it was and how glad I was to discover this restaurant.

"Vlaro's is magical," she said without any kind of immediately discernable accent—certainly not Italian. "I think it's my favorite restaurant in Boston."

"Do you live here?" I asked, looking at her while futilely trying to spear an olive at the same time.

"I do now, but originally I'm from California."

"Really? What part?"

"Near Santa Monica."

"Ah, I used to live near there myself for a while, years ago. Where else have you lived?"

"Some time in Europe," she said, averting her eyes for the first time, "and then for awhile in Philadelphia."

"Really? I lived in Philly, too. In fact I live there now," I said with a little laugh. We then discovered that we were in Philadelphia for a few years at the same time, 14 years ago. Why couldn't I have met her then when I was young enough? I thought. We talked a little more and then she told me her name was Irene and asked if I were dining alone and if so, would I like to join her? I smiled more broadly than I probably should have, thanked her, and moved to her table.

As difficult as it would have been for me to carry on a conversation in a similar situation in my twenties, it was now surprisingly simple and spontaneous. I found out she'd done a variety of interesting things in her life besides the interesting places she'd done them in. She was an actress in local TV commercials and regional theater in California (briefly and in minor roles); an art student in Europe, where she was also an architect's assistant. In fact, she wound up marrying the architect and having a child, a son, who was now a lawyer in Chicago. The marriage ended in divorce. (I pointed out that I'd had one of those, too.) She'd also taught English as a second language in Chicago and was now involved in an import business in Boston that I didn't completely understand.

She talked in a way that compelled my attention, although she rarely raised her voice, which made me listen to her all the more closely.

As a result, I noticed that she skipped over her Philadelphia years, and I was just about to ask her what she did there when she suddenly asked me about my life.

I told her I was a businessman but was, at heart, a frustrated composer.

"A song writer?" she asked.

"No, I'm afraid I mean classical music," I said with a laugh.

"Oh dear God, I'm sorry," she said, laughing herself. "That's the hardest thing in the world to do, even worse than writing plays. Do you teach?" she said.

I told her that I'd gotten involved with computers and made some money there but was now essentially retired. I added that I'd also had a daughter but was now living alone, as I had been for a number of years. To this piece of unremarkable information she merely nodded.

I was seized then by a rather adolescent panic that I had nothing left to say about my doings, which were much less interesting than hers and would happily have resumed my former role of interviewing her, but she continued to ask me questions about myself.

"Can I get any of your pieces on CD?" she said.

I appreciated that she didn't ask if there were any available in stores. "I can just send you some."

"Oh, thanks. That would be great."

"God knows I've got a lot of copies," I said with a laugh. "It was never a very developed thing, my composing. I mean my attempts to have any kind of career with it. More like the road not taken, that I wished I had at least tried to crawl down."

"Still it must have brought you a lot of pleasure too, to create music. What a gift—I can't imagine it."

"I didn't imagine it hard enough was my problem," I said, finishing my drink and then looking around, a bit helplessly, I suppose, for a waitress to order another. Fortunately, in Vlaro, like all successful restaurants, the waitress always arrives very quickly at such times. I was also pleased that Irene ordered another drink as well.

We talked easily for the next few minutes about this and that until suddenly she said, "Paul there's a reason why I talked to you tonight and invited you to eat dinner with me."

I raised my eyebrows and merely said, "Yes?"

"I want to get this out in the open before we talk anymore. I think we've met before."

"What?"

"I think we spent some time together once in Philadelphia years ago. I fact, I'm sure of it."

"I'm sure I would have remembered if we had," I said as convincingly as possible, though in the last half year alone my memory had started to shrink like my signature.

"It wasn't a great deal of time. It was a dinner, or part of one."

"Why do you think this? You have to explain."

"It's nothing I'm proud of. In fact, I'm ashamed and have been for a long time."

"I would have remembered you, someone who looks like you," I blurted.

"I didn't look the same then."

"You are aware that you're very beautiful right now, aren't you?"

"Thank you but I looked different then. My hair was a different color. I was a redhead."

"Still, I mean, I'm sure I would have remembered."

"Maybe there are reasons why you don't want to remember."

Was it that she rejected me or hurt me

in some way after we made love? But it was impossible that I could forget that kind of experience with someone as attractive as her, who could only have been even more attractive years ago.

"I don't see how I could have forgotten you if I met you or why you're so sure you've met me?"

"Well, for one thing you look like the man I remember, and his name was also Paul. And we've already established that we were both in Philadelphia at that time."

I nodded to show that there was some circumstantial evidence.

"Still, Paul is a very common name, and Philadelphia is a big city. And this was, what, ten years ago?"

"Fourteen."

"So, I mean, the odds that it was me are pretty small."

"But it was you. I don't know if you're pretending not to remember out of politeness or…"

"No, I assure you I'm not."

"Anyway, it's important for me that you let me apologize. I thought the second I saw you that it was you. I considered it a miracle so I had to talk to you, and after talking with you about music and other things, I know it's you."

"Can you tell me a little about what you say happened between us?"

"I'm going to need a drink to do that."

I signaled to the waitress, and we waited until it arrived in a kind of suspended animation. Except my thoughts were moving rapidly and I suspect hers were, too. I was feeling a mix of things, mainly a desire for her that astonished me, but also a concern about my memory and her emotional stability that made me dread to hear the story in which I was supposedly mistreated.

At last the drinks came. I took a swallow; she took two and then finally spoke. "It was in a bookstore. The Borders that used to be on 16th and Walnut in Center City."

Borders, I thought, another symbol of the changing and soon-to-be lost world I was already half forgetting.

"You were staring at me."

"So far, completely believable," I interjected with a smile in an effort to make things a little lighter. "But was I really doing it so blatantly? That's not my usual modus operandi."

"Actually, you were staring at me when you thought I wasn't noticing. But then you started following me, and when I went to the pay phone to make a call, you stood behind me as if in line to use it, and I got the feeling that you were listening to my call. Then, sure enough, when I went to the café, you followed behind and sat at the table next to mine, still staring at me whenever you thought I wasn't noticing."

"This really doesn't sound like me," I said.

"But it was you—and you kept doing it at the table. Finally I said, 'Was there something you wanted to say to me? I mean you are sort of following me, aren't you? It's not my imagination?'"

"So, what did I say? Did I deny it, I suppose?"

"No, you didn't deny it. In fact, you admitted it. You said, 'I seem to have a very strong desire to talk to you.'"

"I'm far too shy to talk that way."

"Maybe the you of 2011, when you're obviously a well-mannered gentleman, but you were quite bold then, and frankly it impressed me, the immature me of that time."

"So what did you say to me?"

"I think I looked at my watch and said something like 'I have a couple of minutes. What did you want to say?'"

"At which point, I assume, I was rendered speechless."

"Not at all. You were quite an adept conversationalist and very persuasive, too. In a matter of minutes you talked me into going with you to a very expensive restaurant in Center City called Eden, I think. I don't know if it still exists."

"No, it doesn't."

"Well, it did then. It was a dark, very chi-chi place lit by candles. We ordered drinks and soon after you began to persuade me to have dinner with you. And that's when you started to do it."

"Do what?"

"You started to show me that you had a lot of money."

"How did I do that?"

"By taking a thick wad of bills out of your pocket or else out of your wallet. And you did it a number of times while we talked. Almost as if you were flashing me."

"This is getting very embarrassing. Besides, I thought you were the villain in this story."

"I was," she said, looking down contritely at the table. "Anyway, I thought you were obviously trying to make an impression on me with your stash of money. And the weird thing was, at the time, it did. I was impressed with your conversation, too, although that was a little weird as well."

"What was I talking about? You can't possibly remember that."

"Not word for word but you were talking about how the Internet is a lie."

"Well that turned out to be true."

"And then how there was no such thing as absolute reality, that we could only know how our brains perceived things, and because of the limitation in how they were programmed, we had no real idea of what time or space really were, or something like that."

"What a dreadful bore I was."

"I didn't find it boring, I was impressed, like I was about your money—but I didn't want to show you how impressed I was so I made some smart ass remark like 'I don't have the time to think about time. I'm too worried about money.' And that's when you did it. You invited me to dinner again and then you took out one of your hundred dollar bills and asked me if I would accept it as a gift so I would worry a little less about money. I was shocked. I said, 'this is very strange, Paul. You assume that I'll take it.'"

"I assume nothing. It's only a little gift," you said.

"And what do you think this is buying?"

"'Nothing at all,' you said. 'I put money on the table to take money off the table of our discussion. It's really just a little gift. Please don't refuse it.' And sad to say, I took it."

I looked closely at her and saw tears forming in her eyes. Though she'd accused me of not wanting to remember, I was actually straining to remember, with mixed results. (Lately when names or places I was trying to recall were on the tip of my tongue but couldn't quite surface, a panic of a kind would start to overwhelm me, and I'd force myself to stop trying to remember anymore or even think about it again.) I began to worry now that that type of panic would happen again.

"Was that it then?" I said as sympathetically as I could.

"No, that was just how it began. You started to tell me a story about a woman who had left you which ultimately became a story about how your mother mistreated you throughout your childhood."

"How did she mistreat me?"

"She was jealous and possessive and overly

flirtatious with you. She managed to make you see her naked many times, you told me. Anyway, at certain key parts or after certain parts that were difficult for you, you continued to slide 50 or 100 dollar bills in my direction and, God help me, I continued to take them."

"What a foolish way to behave," I said, "if it was me."

"What? You still don't remember?"

"If you're sure it was me, I think you're probably right."

"How else could I know about your mother?"

I bowed my head and said nothing.

"Were you in the habit then of paying women to listen to you?" she added.

"I've paid women one way or another to listen to me my whole life though I can't say I remember doing it as overtly as you described. I do know I was drinking a lot at that time in my life, which could explain why I don't remember it now and may not have remembered it then the next morning. I mean, when it was over I probably went home and drank away my embarrassment."

"It was a lot worse than embarrassment, what I did. You see the longer I listened to you, the more money you kept paying me and the less I protested until I didn't protest at all. By the time your story ended, I had almost five hundred dollars. I'd felt a lot of emotions listening to you talk. I felt sorry for you, I did, especially for the things your mother did to you, but I was also increasingly nervous about being with you when the dinner ended, still convinced, your assurances to the contrary, that when it ended and you realized how much money you'd given me, you'd expect certain things from me that I wasn't ready to do and that would make you very angry."

"All of this is perfectly understandable," I

said. "I mean you didn't ask or expect to have to listen to my monologue when you agreed to go to dinner with me. You didn't expect I'd keep thrusting money at you either. I fail to see your crime, regardless of how the evening ended."

"Let me tell you how it ended. Your drinking finally caught up with you, and you excused yourself to use the men's room. It was the first time since I met you that I was alone, and I was still convinced that you'd ask me to go to bed and get angry when I'd tell you no. I was somewhat physically intimidated by you, although you weren't a large man, and I didn't think you'd physically attack me. But I did think then that you'd demand your money back, and I didn't want to give it back."

"Why should you? I gave it to you as a gift. At any rate, I'm sure you worked harder for it than any of the therapists I'd been intermittently seeing then."

"So, that's the story. While you were in the men's room I left the restaurant with your money in my purse. Later, when the guilt got too bad I vowed to give the money to charity. I thought I'd sponsor one of those third-world, poverty-stricken children I'd seen on TV. But I never did that either. Instead I spent it on clothes and make-up for the most part, just like a prostitute would. I didn't even spend it on my son."

She put her hands to her eyes and started crying.

"I'm sorry," she said, taking her hands away from her eyes at last. "Now I've ruined a second dinner for you."

"You haven't ruined anything. You've made me feel my past and part of my, well, 'extended youth,' shall we say and who can put a price on that?" I said as the waitress approached me with the bill.

"Oh no, you're not going to pay again."

"Please, I already have."

"At least let me pay my share," she said, beginning to rummage through her oversized purse.

"Please, Irene, don't embarrass me."

When this little pseudo 'argument' ended she excused herself to 'freshen up' in the ladies room. It occurred to me that I could now avenge myself and desert her and that she may have given me the chance on purpose, but I never seriously considered it. In fact, as soon as she returned I excused myself to go to the men's room thus giving her the same chance which about half of me believed she'd take. But she didn't. Instead, when I sat down again, she said, "Would you like to have some coffee and a yummy strawberry cheesecake at my place? I live in the Prudential building, it's not a long walk at all."

When I accepted, it was as if I was 45 again, eager, of course, for whatever the evening would bring my way with such an attractive woman. But after we walked a block or so I started to worry. What if she expected a sexual conclusion to the evening? Normally I wouldn't expect that from a woman these days, but given our special circumstances and her ostensible desire to make things up to me (plus what I sensed was a penchant on her part to be excited by odd situations) it was entirely possible. What would I say or do then? I hadn't even brought my Viagra with me on this trip so I possibly wouldn't be able to do anything. She already knew I was unmarried and hadn't any special woman in my life so I couldn't use the 'I'm being faithful to my girlfriend' excuse. Amazing how I'd let myself get into this situation so blindly. How I had first reacted before I saw the situation as it was.

The walk seemed to take place in a dreamtime,

being much quicker than it really was. One moment I was in the plant-surrounded half darkness of the underground restaurant, the next I was nodding at her doorman, who seemed to have a bemused smile as we walked into the elevator en route to her apartment.

Her apartment was small but expensive. There was thick off-white, wall-to-wall carpeting, an impressive view of Boston from her living room, some pretty nice art and other artifacts on her walls. She served me the cheesecake as advertised but instead of coffee offered me wine.

"Your home is lovely," I said, as I sat down on her green sofa that appeared to be velvet. I placed my drink on a coaster on top of the table in front of us as she thanked me for the compliment. She was seated on the sofa, too, but two or three feet from me. I was planning my departure in 20 to 30 minutes.

"That's really nice of you to say. I've always been insecure about my ability to decorate."

"I don't see why," I said, scanning the room again for something I might have missed. All the other chairs in the room were velvet, too. I stared at them for a while.

"What are you thinking?" she asked, a seemingly polite question I'd grown to dislike over the years.

"I was thinking all your furniture is blue or green—an unusual but really cool color scheme. It made me think of the piece "Blue in Green" by the jazz pianist Bill Evans."

She put down her now empty glass with some emphasis.

"I was always so intrigued by jazz and always wished I could meet someone really knowledgeable who could help explain it to me. And ironically I met you, years ago, who already was that person, with a whole lot more to offer, too, and I walked out on you without a word of warning."

I felt a flash of anger when she said it that way, but I was worried she might cry again so I said with largely faux enthusiasm, "Hey, we forgot to have a toast."

"Good idea," she said, as she poured herself a second glass of wine and refilled half of mine.

"To reunions of old friends and to new beginnings," she said, just before our glasses clinked.

I decided again that it didn't matter what happened so long ago between us and moreover shouldn't matter anymore what had happened between my mother and me either. After all, my mother had died years ago, and I rarely spent any time remembering her, though I did still dream about her from time to time. But to use her as a crutch or explanation for my various failures and frustrations such as my being alone now or my not pursuing a career in music was ridiculous and, at this stage of my life, pathetic. There were still things I could do to improve my life despite my diminishing powers. I could, for example, become more aggressive about getting in touch with my daughter. I could simply book a flight and visit her.

While I was immersed in this line of thought, I somehow managed to continue my conversation with Irene mainly by asking her about her relationship with her ex-husband. She may have been unusual in many ways, but like most women I'd met, once asked, she couldn't resist talking in considerable detail about the man she'd divorced. This is how I'll fill up my twenty-five minutes, I thought, by being a good listener and nothing more disturbing than the very odd coincidence of meeting her would ever happen.

But I'd miscalculated the power of her emotions—a mistake I'd made with women before as well. Irene was openly crying again, and there was no way I could pretend it wasn't happening and just wait it out. On the other hand, I had no idea what to say or do. As if sensing my dilemma she finally said, "Paul, I'm sorry to carry on like this."

"No, it's fine, don't worry about it. I understand."

"It appears I've invited you up for the world's saddest cup of coffee."

I laughed a little in another futile effort to lighten things, resisting the temptation to mention that so far coffee had yet to make an appearance.

"You're really so kind," she suddenly said while moving a little closer to me on the sofa. "Do you think you could just give me a little friendship hug?"

Of course, I did, I had to, though it had been so long since I'd hugged an attractive woman in this kind of situation. To make matters more confusing I felt some stirrings, something that rarely happened to me without Viagra. But I pulled away just after we exchanged a kiss short enough that I could pretend it was merely a gesture of friendship.

"You really are so nice. It appears I've mistreated the kindest man I've ever met."

"No, no," was all I could stupidly mutter.

"Yes, yes, I know better...now."

As I feared she poured herself another drink, which she attacked right away.

"Paul, you must tell me something important about yourself now to make things more equal between us. Something about your ex-wife or about your mother. You said your mother flirted with you all the time in ways that really hurt you. Tell me some story about her so I can feel closer to you."

I felt angry again in a way that mystified me. Suddenly I was thinking about how Irene walked off with my money years ago. How tricked and humiliated I must have felt.

"Paul, have I said something wrong?"

"No, I just don't feel like talking about my mother now."

"Of course not. It was a stupid thing for me to say."

She looked closely at me as if waiting for me to contradict her again and make her feel better. In that respect she did remind me of my mother, but I stayed silent and let the statement stand. Then she put her hand on me just above my knee.

"Can you think of any other way we can get close?"

She had bent forward, and I could see much more of her cleavage. It was very inviting. (She was a sneaky one and had probably undone one button from her purple top when I wasn't looking.) She did a lot of things when I wasn't looking—that was her modus operandi. She was like my mother that way, too, come to think of it.

"I'm pretty tired so I think I better be getting home," I said.

She removed her hand quickly as if she'd burned it. "Okay Paul, I see how it is. You wouldn't even have a drink."

"I had a drink. I had two drinks."

"You wouldn't even give us a chance because 14 years ago I was a bad girl."

Would you screw someone who robbed you? I wanted to say but didn't.

"Your forgiveness only goes so far, I guess. You've obviously measured out how much you could give and found that you've hit your limit. You're just like my ex that way and like my father too, who'd ration out his kisses like a bill he had to pay. One on the forehead for my birthday and nothing more. Why are all you men (that word was said with sarcastic emphasis) so goddamn stingy?" she said, standing up and pointing her finger at me.

"I'm going," I said, getting up from the couch myself.

"Yes, flee the wicked, witch woman. Escape with all your money before she kisses you again."

There was more that she said, but I shut the door against it.

Outside, on the street it was dark, at first, and then bright—with a wind that was both strong and hot. I felt temporarily disoriented as I do when I'm trying to remember something but can't bring it into focus. They say people will do anything to avoid certain memories, but the truth is if our memory went, our sanity would explode in a moment. Besides, I wanted to remember Irene and my mother too, otherwise the same thing might happen to me again. We aren't built to withstand the same humiliation twice, neither the old nor the young—it's just too much for us.

The next morning I took an uneventful plane ride home to Philadelphia thinking of Irene the whole time.

HIDE ISLAND

When she felt he wouldn't notice, she turned slightly to her left and looked out the large picture window. The bay was still but enormous clouds pierced by a few crayon-like streaks of sun were massing over the water. Outside there was a fairly strong wind, but she could barely hear it, only see some rare white caps on the water.

They were sitting in parallel reclining chairs not close enough to touch without an effort although with Mr. R (as she called him to herself) she had nothing to worry about anyway since he had no interest in her that way. He'd answered her ad eagerly in the Gulfport Gabber for a domestic helper for his condominium, but unlike a few of her former clients, had never made a pass at her. Instead, he simply wanted to talk, each day giving her less actual domestic work to do. He talked mostly about his son, Chris, who he was talking about again now in an almost ghostly voice that grew softer as each sentence progressed until it was almost a whisper.

"Did I tell you the story he made up called 'Hide Island'?"

"No, you didn't," she said.

"It takes place not too far from here along the coast of southern Georgia."

She nodded to feign interest, then, realizing he may have missed it, turned toward him and nodded again.

"A family of four called the Culversons was going on a vacation and came to a fork in the road. On the left was a sign that said "To Jeckell Island," and on the right was a sign pointing to "Hide Island." The family, who had all read the book, thought this misspelling was funny.

"Well, I guess if we know what's good for us, the choice is obvious," the mother said with a laugh, "Jeckell Island, here we come."

"By the way," Mr. R said, "there really is a Jeckell Island that's a center for ecological study and tourism of a kind. Anyhow, Mrs. Culverson's son said, 'Jeckell Island sounds so lame, and we know what it is anyway. Let's go to Hide Island instead. It's probably got a haunted house or a water park.'"

The mention of the word "water park" was all it took for his younger sister, Candy Culverson, to adopt his cause, and soon the Culversons were heading toward Hide Island."

She snuck a look at her watch while he was clearing his throat. Ruth always got so angry when she was late. Sometimes Justine felt being at Mr. R's was the easiest money she'd ever made, but other times she wanted to quit because her job, while physically easy, was emotionally draining. She felt anxious about people or situations she didn't understand, and she didn't understand Mr. R and his relationship with Chris. Of course, she realized Chris was dead but Mr. R had only said that once and so softly and seemingly long ago it was as if she'd imagined or dreamed it.

"As soon as the Culversons stopped at the town's only restaurant for lunch," Mr. Richardson continued, "they began to notice how odd all the customers looked. Almost all of them wore black hoods or masks that completely covered their faces. Those people whose faces weren't covered had a chalky, bleached-out quality to their skin, yet they lurched about energetically enough and few of them were skinny."

"What the Culversons began to discover was that Hide Island was populated almost exclusively by a new kind of zombie created by the island's governor, Dr. Franklin Hide, whose laboratory (and ultimate hiding place) was located in a vast underground cave. For security reasons, Dr. Hide had bred a species of both trees and plants that grew extraordinarily thick leaves and completely covered his cave. Inside the cave, in his laboratory, he trained his creations to fit in with the 'human population' of Hide Island."

"Why did Dr. Hide advertise Hide Island, albeit secretively, leaving that sign in the fork in the road that lured the Culversons? Precisely to entice them because Hide's zombies, and Dr. Hide, himself, needed to be fed," Mr. Richardson said with a slight smile at the corners of his thin lips. "Of course, that's just the bare-bones version. All of his stories were incredibly detailed."

Perhaps she should now introduce the subject of her leaving while he was in a relatively good mood. It was too cold to swim today, but she could picture herself in Vinoy Park looking out at the bay where the water was sometimes brilliant blue and unruffled and the sand was white and clean. It made her feel peaceful sometimes and then, of course, there were her plans to meet Ruth.

"So, what did you think of Chris's story?" Mr. R. said, turning to face her with his big hazel eyes opened wide. When they looked like that, his eyes made her nervous. Her father had often looked at her that way.

"I liked it. Was it meant to be a horror story or to be funny, too?"

"I think both. I think it was meant to be scary and funny, just like life is. Chris was fond of mixing genres, even when he was a child."

"He was amazingly creative," she noted, thinking of all the stories Chris apparently made up; she guessed she meant what she said.

Mr. R looked half sad, half mystified. "It was almost like a replacement world he entered for a good part of every day. But look at this world," he said, suddenly gesturing with both arms. "Can you blame him? Is it hard to understand?"

"No," she said. She knew enough to agree, knew it instinctively by now, though there'd been times in her job when she'd created some tense moments with a client simply by expressing a different point of view which too often lay the groundwork for an argument. Unfortunately, these arguments sometimes escalated and once resulted in her losing a job. Yet, in spite of this, she found herself too often disagreeing with Mr. R (silently this time, thank God) without knowing why. And though she'd just shown herself that she had the impulse pretty well under control, it was disturbing to know that it still existed.

"I saw a boy who looked like Chris the other day," Mr. R said.

"Really?"

"I went to St. Petersburg Beach to take a walk—Chris used to love it there—and I saw this boy at the Don Caesar hotel. We had a very nice conversation."

She nodded, thinking, oh God, here comes

the confession. She, herself, had once worked as a maid in that hotel (the most expensive one on the beach), which was a gold mine for certain kinds of specialty hookers.

"How old was he?" she blurted.

She saw Mr. Richardson's face redden slightly. "He said he was 18."

"Was he?"

"Well, I don't know. I didn't ask him for his I.D. Why are you asking me that?"

"No reason." She said quickly. "What's his name?"

"Emilio, I think you'd like him."

"Is he Hispanic?"

"I suppose. Once again I didn't check his I.D. I didn't know St. Petersburg beach was a hot spot for illegal aliens. I suppose I should have checked your I.D. before hiring you, Justine."

"You could."

"Well, I don't believe in IDs. Do you really think we can identify ourselves in this world?"

It was one of his statements that she couldn't answer right away, if ever. She could only blink a few times then make a semi-supportive sound that stopped just short of being a word. What did he want from her? She couldn't quite grasp it. She used to wonder the same thing about her father until she slowly found out. It was the way of the world, she supposed. By talking less, men made themselves more mysterious and frightening.

"Chris said that 'Hide Island' should be a movie, and I agreed with him," Mr. Richardson said with another slight smile. He was looking out the window now as well, perhaps at the sailboat that passed by. "There's a very strong visual component to the story, what with the zombies and the thick green plants and the sea. Don't you agree?"

"Yes, I do."

"He also thought there should be a sequel to it that would focus on Dr. Hide's development of a master race of zombies, as well as settling the fate of those poor devils, the Culversons."

He went on to tell her the story of the sequel that segued somehow into a real trip to Madrid that he and Chris took years ago. It seemed the two of them had traveled to half the world. Mr. Richardson, himself, had said that by the time Chris was 12, he'd already been to ten countries and four continents. He was describing a game Chris would play with the pigeons in Sol, which she gathered was the kind of Times Square of Madrid, when she saw him look at his watch and say, "I think Emilio likes to travel, too," and as if that observation settled some issue in their conversation, which it didn't, he suddenly rose from his reclining chair, thanked her profusely for coming to see him and began to write her a check.

"So what is it that scares you about him?" Ruth said, turning toward her. They were sitting on a bench in Vinoy Park facing the bay. As soon as she asked the question, Ruth put her hand on Justine's thigh, but Justine didn't respond. Ruth had started freelance hooking the last few months but today was dressed as a civilian. They'd met a half-year ago at a hair styling class from which both eventually dropped out.

"I don't know," Justine finally said.

"Did he come on to you?"

"No, never. He just wants to talk to me and maybe have me clean a little. He hates to wash dishes."

Ruth laughed. "Nothing unusual there. How old is he, anyway?"

"Hard to say. He colors his hair. He could be anywhere from his early to late sixties."

"Well be thankful. It sounds like easy money to me. I just don't like that he keeps you so long."

"The money isn't the problem."

"So what is it?" Ruth said, pushing back some windblown strands of her dark-brown hair, the approximate color of Justine's. There was still a strong, late December breeze though it was almost 70 degrees out. Justine looked away from her for a moment, following the path of a crane that scurried by.

"I don't know, he talks about his son all the time, who I think is dead but he never refers to him as dead, except maybe once, and lately he's talking about this other boy he just met. I'm starting to think he might be some kind of pedophile, that he's on the verge of telling me."

"Shit."

"Yeah, really."

"Well, if he ever tells you that just keep your cool, finish your day, and collect your paycheck but don't go back there. I had a client once who used to tell me he killed his wife, strangled her to death, but he always told me while he was doing me so I figured he was saying it to help himself get off, you know? But then he started to tell me more and I broke it off. I was scared shitless for a while thinking he might hunt me down cause of what he'd told me. Ended with my moving to St. Pete right around when I started seeing you."

"He didn't know your name?"

"Course not. I did some work on my face (not just because of him) when I moved, too, and turned my hair a new color. I still get the creeps thinking about him. So if this guy ever says anything bad, just drop him before he drops you."

"But he hasn't done anything bad, yet."

"Yeah, they never do until they do, you know? I know he's paying you good. Jesus, I hope he's paying you top dollar. I really do. Just watch out. I don't want to lose you, okay?"

She couldn't have expected anything else from Ruth. How could she think Ruth could understand someone she'd never met, someone that she herself found completely mystifying. She only knew it wasn't one thing she could point to about Mr. R, much less ever prove in a court of law. It was more like an ever-shifting collage of impressions or sometimes just expressions that crossed his face when he was talking about Chris or lately, Emilio.

Other times it was just the way he looked when he didn't think she was watching him, a subtle or not so subtle expression of guilt or regret. And then, of course, there were the grand philosophical statements he made (the conversation stoppers she called them to herself). She could never quite tell if they meant something profound or nothing at all. (It was often that way with college professors, she thought, which Mr. R had been.) Statements like, "I don't have any time of my own—it's the world's time, I'm just a temporary user of it" or worse than that, "if our species could just rid itself of all religions, and truly experience a collective realization of our inevitable death it could be the clearest path towards universal compassion." She wouldn't even bother to tell that one to Ruth.

She was loading the final two glasses into his dishwasher when she felt him looking at her again. There were photographs of Chris all over the kitchen, as there were throughout the condominium, and he could always claim to be looking at them. But she knew this time he wasn't. It had started that way with her father, too. His sneaking cryptic looks at her while the two of them ate breakfast alone or sometimes she'd feel it when she was walking downstairs, and she'd look and he'd be watching her from an indirect angle, holding a cell phone or some other prop but still watching her. It was shortly after that that she began seeing him half nude or sometimes more than that virtually every day. He'd "forget" to close the bathroom door when he stepped out of the shower. The angle of the door would be set just wide enough so she couldn't miss him. Then it started to happen in a similar way when he got dressed in his bedroom. Always the mirrored door was at just the right angle to make her see. Nothing she could ever prove though. A game of angles and split seconds and "coincidences" that could go on to infinity.

"Mr. Richardson, did you want something?" she said, walking back towards the chairs in his living room where he was pacing as if waiting for her to resume talking with him. Mr. Richardson paced more than anyone she'd ever known. The question, of course, was why.

This time it was to tell her another of Chris's stories. There were still more framed photographs and paintings of, and by, Chris on the living room walls in about the same proportion as there were in the bedrooms, kitchen and bathroom. She forgot to tell Ruth about this, that Mr. Richardson's home was like a museum of his son, if Chris really was his son. She should have told Ruth that and couldn't figure out why she hadn't.

...They were seated in the reclining chairs facing the bay again as Mr. Richardson's soft, yet oddly precise voice floated up to her.

"This is one of Chris' most original stories, I think. It's about a local T.V. weatherman of less than average ability whose ratings are starting to slip to the point where he's about to get fired. Suddenly a grand yet hidden force of nature called the King of the Clouds intervenes and gives him the power not only to predict weather but to create it. For a while the weatherman does the right thing and creates worldwide good weather. The world rejoices but the weatherman gets no credit for the higher ratings. It's only when he creates and then correctly predicts a series of terrible storms that no other weatherman does that his ratings, and renown, skyrocket but at the cost of terrible suffering to humanity."

She looked at Mr. Richardson. His face was stricken with emotion as if he were narrating a true story.

"How does the story end?" she said.

"The King of the Clouds realizes it made a terrible mistake and starts to hunt down the greedy weatherman. It's hard to outrun a force of nature, impossible really, as Chris pointed out—he was only 13 when he wrote it—so eventually the weatherman is sucked up by a tornado and disintegrates."

"Pretty gruesome ending."

"Yes, I guess it is, but he told it with such smiling eyes that it seemed more like a fairy tale, a Grimm Brothers one perhaps, but he saw it as a cautionary tale about using power wisely. He wanted that story to be made into a movie, too."

She took another quick look at him while the sun set over the bay. Mr. R was dabbing at his eyes. I'm a monster, she thought briefly. He's crying for his son who he loved. Still a part of her wanted to be sure. She'd been right about her father after all. She looked out at the bay again thinking, I'm being paid to sit in silence and look out the window while an old man tries to stop crying.

"I've kept you too long today," he finally said, "I've told you too many of his stories."

"That's okay. I like to listen to them."

"Chris was so funny and full of life, jumping up and laughing as he told his stories."

"You always speak of him in the past tense," she suddenly said.

"Because he died, Justine. Didn't I tell you that? The present is for the living, don't you think? Otherwise things would get too crowded," he added, forcing a little laugh.

He'd said it clearly now, and she hated herself again for suspecting him. She was always suspecting the worst in people, she knew. Yet she'd also had a number of her suspicions confirmed. She'd been right about her father, in essence anyway, though he'd never done anything physically to her. And she was right about Ruth hooking, knew it at least two weeks before Ruth finally told her in bed. Was right also about how jealous and possessive Ruth was, too. Felt it and then saw her going through the papers on her desk the next day, and a week later going through her pocketbook. Ironically enough, since she started to hook, Ruth was more jealous and suspicious than ever. So how was she supposed to believe Mr. R or at least believe him right away? It was hard to think about because it was awful, but children died before their parents all the time. Of course, she didn't know how Chris died, but she couldn't ask Mr. R that. She'd have to wait till he wanted to talk about it, she supposed.

Mr. Richardson was pouring himself a glass of wine from a bottle she hadn't noticed. She thought of Ruth in the park touching her like she owned her. It was too much to deal with, her hooking, too dangerous with all the diseases around and too painful emotionally, though Ruth kept saying, "it doesn't count because they're men."

"Are you all right dear? Have I made you sad?" Mr. Richardson said.

She was crying softly but didn't think he'd noticed. A while sailboat passed by while two crows flew beside it, as if guiding its passage.

"I'm all right," she said. "I feel terrible for your loss."

"It's part of the nature of things, isn't it? I don't really know why humans alone were given death or the knowledge of it—same thing really. It's the principle crime of nature, isn't it. Though a poet said, 'death is the mother of beauty,' I wonder if he ever lost a young son."

She took a swallow of her drink. She remembered then that Mr. Richardson had been an English professor and wondered briefly what it would be like to be in his class. Ruth told her it was a waste of time, but she still wished she'd finished college.

"How long ago did it happen?"

He refilled his empty glass on the Formica table by his chair.

"Would you like another, too? I see you're empty."

"Sure," she said.

After a couple of swallows he said, "For a long time I didn't want to live and was quite sure I wouldn't, yet for some reason I did. Actually, my health has been problematical ever since Chris was born. I think having to raise him as a single parent kept me going, demanding though it was."

"Was his mother able to..."

"His mother loved him and was a good woman, but we divorced when Chris was only one or two. We shared him but we no longer talk now. It's just too difficult."

She watched him finish his second glass and then she all but finished hers. She noticed he had large, almond-shaped eyes like she did.

She'd always been struck by how little she looked like her father.

"But I'm talking far too much. Tell me some more about your life, please. I want to hear."

She thought of her job, the elderly people she shopped and washed dishes for all of whom had spouses who had died, though none grieved the way Mr. R did. What a job she had! The only way she could get more money would be if she took a nursing course and then could charge her clients more. But that kind of nursing involved a lot of unpleasant things she didn't think she could bear to do.

"Do you mind my asking if you're in a relationship of some kind?" he said.

"No, I don't mind your asking. I am, kind of, but there are problems."

He nodded sympathetically, no doubt expecting more, but she cut herself short.

"If you ever feel like talking I'm all ears. Sometimes I think listening to other lives has saved me from my own."

"Thank you, Mr. Richardson."

"Please call me Jason."

"Okay, Jason."

"I want to give you something besides your check," he said, walking towards his bedroom.

It will be a photograph of Chris, she thought, or else one of Chris's drawings. When he returned, Mr. R was moving slower than he usually did, as if he were walking in his sleep.

"I'd like you to have a key to my place," he said, opening his hand. The key seemed to gleam as he placed it in her palm. "Just in case you're ever in trouble, or need something, or just want to talk, you can come here. You're always welcome. Think of it as your own, more benevolent, Hide Island. Sometimes I unplug the phone so I can sleep. My heart isn't what it used to be, well, my whole body isn't, and I find that I'm sleeping more than ever. So that's why I'd like you to have a copy of my key, Justine, so you can come over whether I hear the phone or not."

She barely had time to say thank you when her cell phone started ringing.

"Sorry," she said. "I should probably answer."

"Of course, what are phone calls but prayers waiting to be answered."

"Where are you?" It was Ruth. Justine walked towards the kitchen before she spoke not wanting Mr. R to hear her. I'm working," she said.

"So get your gorgeous ass over here, okay? I thought your job ended at five."

"It does but he started talking. He needed to talk about something."

"What about what I need? Have you forgotten about me?"

"No, of course not."

"He better be paying you overtime for this."

"He will."

"He's not supposed to get you for free, I am."

"I know, but the thing is..."

"No, the thing is I'm all alone now. I've been letting men come in my mouth all day, and I don't have anything decent to smoke or drink and you're supposed to be here to hold me. Isn't that what you said you'd always do?"

"Yes, but I'm not feeling very good either. My stomach hurts and..."

"So come over and talk to me and we'll get drunk together. You know I know how to make you feel good."

"No, Ruth I can't. I really don't feel up to it tonight. I'm sorry," she said and a half-minute later hung up the phone.

*   *   *

Ruth was like the Florida weather, there was always the possibility of a storm. She wasn't surprised to see the next morning that Ruth had called her four more times during the night. Good thing she'd turned off the ringer. She listened to the first message or rather a small part of it. Ruth's voice was loud, angry, demanding, but Justine didn't return her call. She was starting to pace as she thought about how easy it would be for Ruth to come over and find her and force some kind of confrontation. Suddenly, she walked out heading for the pier and wound up walking through Vinoy Park again. There was little chance that Ruth would look for her there. Eventually, the drugs Ruth took would wear off and Ruth would sleep until one or two, or so Justine thought when she first went to the park. But after sitting on a bench for 15 minutes she began to worry what would happen if Ruth were on speed or coke. What if, in her rage, she decided not to sleep at all or only for a few hours, then decided to try to track her down? If that were the case, the park might be one of the first places she would check.

She got up from the bench and headed back to the Bay Front, suddenly feeling tremendously exposed. She decided to go inside the St. Petersburg Library—the least likely place Ruth would go to try to find her.

Taking a magazine at random from the rack, she sat down at a table in a far corner and tried to read it. Only then did she notice she'd taken Time magazine, which made her think of Mr. R's remark about time—that it belonged to the world and he was "just a temporary user of it." She had to laugh for a second. Wasn't she living out, in a way, Chris's story "Hide Island" this morning, lurching about from place to place pursuing safety the way the zombies were pursuing food in the form of people?

She wondered then if she should visit Mr. R and pushing aside the magazine began a frantic search through her pocketbook. While she looked she saw images of his long, kind, mysterious face. Saw again the view of the bay from his condo with its sailboats and silence. Finally, at the bottom of her bag she found it—the glittering new key to Hide Island.

The clouds were gathering over the bay again. She saw them from the balcony after the elevator took her to the third floor. Once more there were odd steaks of orange, purple and pink, as well as colors that there were no words for, that seemed to infiltrate the clouds at random. She wondered if the King of the Clouds would be pleased with the arrangement.

Am I really doing this? She thought when she reached his door. But apparently she was because after a moment's hesitation, she withdrew her key, and after trying it a few times the door to his condominium suddenly opened.

She heard something before she saw it. It was the sound of feet running lightly but rapidly in the condominium. There were no lights on and almost all the blinds had been shut, blocking out most of the evening light. She felt her heart beat and wondered if she should turn around and run for the door. But the person, who looked to be running in circles might have a gun and for all she knew might shoot her in the back.

She turned on the hallway light and saw that the runner was young, in fact a boy. For a moment, she thought it was Chris, that Mr. Richardson had been lying or speaking metaphorically in a very strange way about his death and was now once again united with his beloved son. But as she took a couple of tentative steps forward she saw that it wasn't Chris, but another boy audibly panting as he continued to run in his frantic circles.

"Hello," she said and then repeated it as she moved closer.

Finally, the boy stopped running and looked at her with an expression of horrified astonishment.

"I didn't do nothing," he said. "I didn't do nothing."

The boy was on the short side and quite skinny with dark hair and matching eyes. She guessed him to be 13 or 14.

"What's your name?"

"Emilio," he said, still running, albeit at a slower speed.

"Where's Mr. Richardson?"

Emilio pointed in the dark towards what used to be Chris's room. "I didn't touch him. I didn't do nothing." She felt her knees buckle as she turned on the chandelier in the living room.

"Who are you?" Emilio said. He had a slight accent the way she'd imagined he would when Mr. R first told her about him.

"I'm his housekeeper," she said. "What happened here?"

She could see fear massing in his eyes the way clouds were in the sky.

"He's in there," he said.

She turned her back on him then, as she walked into the room.

Mr. Richardson lay on the bed, unmoving like a small hill on a dark plain, she thought, then more like a little wave that somehow stopped before it could break.

She knew immediately but then just as quickly decided that she didn't know.

"Mr. Richardson." She said his name twice, three times and then again, "Mr. Richardson, are you all right?"

Although she didn't want to, she forced herself to turn on the desk lamp. He was still lying on his back without moving. She only dared to look at his face for a few seconds. It was pale and rigid with a faint bluish color in his cheeks—a color she'd never seen before.

She reached out to touch the lower part of his leg, then forced herself to tap his knees several times but he stayed still. She looked up then and saw Emilio standing in the doorway, silent and vigilant as if listening closely for a word from her that would magically change everything.

"Is he dead?" he finally asked. It was as though he'd asked, "Is he still dead?" as if death were somehow a reversible condition like taking a nap.

She stood up and looked at him.

"Yes he is. Now you have to tell me what happened."

"I didn't do nothing."

"How long have you been here?"

"Twenty, thirty minutes. He was like this when I came over."

"How did you get in here?" she asked, feeling increasingly as if Mr. Richardson was somehow listening to her and judging her competence.

"The door was unlocked when I got here."

That was possibly true. He'd sometimes left the door open when she came over to work before giving her the key.

"So how did you get here? You don't drive do you? You don't look old enough to drive."

He didn't answer and shuffled his feet.

"Did he pick you up at the beach and give you a ride here?"

"No, no it wasn't like that."

"How did you get here then?"

"I took a cab."

"From St. Petersburg Beach? That's kind of expensive isn't it?"

"Mr. Richardson paid for it."

"How'd he do that?"

"With his credit card."

She looked at his eyes closely again. "So when you came in you saw him like this?"

"Yes, he was lying still."

"Did you try to get him up?"

"Yes, I said his name a lot but he didn't move."

"Did you touch him to try to get him up?"

He looked down at the floor. "Yes, I touch him a little but he didn't move."

Were you used to touching him? She wanted to ask. Were you paid to touch him when you came over? Were you told to say your name was Chris? Instead she waited till their eyes met. His clothes were on the shabby side and smelled a little. "I'm going to call the police," she said. "Why don't you go now, if you want. Do you want to go now?"

"Yes," he said, nodding vigorously.

"Do you know how to get back to St. Petersburg Beach?"

"Yes, I know."

"You have enough money to get home?"

"Yes, I think so."

She took a ten-dollar bill out of her purse and handed it to him. "You sure? You know where the bus is?"

"I know a man in Gulfport, I can stay with him."

"Here in Gulfport?"

"Yes, in another condo."

"You sure he's home?"

"Yes, I call him already. I'll go there now,

okay?" he said to her as if she were his mother, while putting her money in the pocket of his faded and frayed pink shirt.

She nodded. "Okay," she said as he ran down the hallway. It seemed inevitable that he would go, so inevitable that she immediately forgot that she'd let him leave. At first for some reason he reminded her of herself, but after she called 911 she thought he reminded her of her mother. Every time she saw her father, her mother was missing, had, in effect, deserted the scene the same way Emilio did, if that were even his real name. She wondered vaguely what his friend in the condominium complex called him. Then she wondered if she should hate Mr. Richardson, but could she even be sure of what he did, and didn't you have to be sure of that before you hated someone? Emilio might have known what happened but for some reason she had let him go. She thought, I don't know how Mr. Richardson lived or died and wondered if the same thing would one day be said about her.

She was pacing in the living room feeling blinded by the maze of smiling photographs and paintings, remembering how Mr. R had once paced there, too. The sound of a siren suddenly stopped her. She froze for a moment before running to the kitchen window where she saw an ambulance and behind it the whirling lights, like colors torn from the sky, of two police cars.

THE ESCORT

A man had started talking to him from the next seat in the bar at Terminal C. The man was friendly at first until he said "I've seen you here before."

"Really?" Kane said, focusing more intently on the man's face with its narrow, slit-like eyes, which, until five minutes before, he'd never seen.

"You travel a lot?"

"No, not a lot," Kane said.

"I ask because I've seen you here a number of times."

"Must have been someone else."

"No, no, I'm sure it was you."

Kane shrugged. "I really don't see how."

The man smiled. His slit-like eyes were green yet strangely unanimated. "You like airports a lot, don't you."

"Excuse me?"

"Do you especially like this airport?"

"The airport's okay, sure."

"I've seen you spending a lot of time in

this part of the airport in particular. Always in Terminal C."

"This part?"

"Yes, from Chili's down to the Men's Room."

"Do you work here?" Kane blurted, immediately regretting that in all likelihood he'd now prolonged the conversation.

"I spend a lot of time here, too. That's why I thought you'd remember me."

"No, nope. Never saw you before," Kane said. He was starting to feel a little nervous as Slit Eyes continued to speak in riddles.

"You really don't?"

"No, nope. I don't really know what you're talking about."

"You know the expression 'ignorance of the law is no excuse'?"

"I think everyone does."

"Well, it isn't, is it? It isn't an excuse."

"Have I broken the law?"

Slit Eyes didn't answer immediately, which made Kane still more anxious.

"There are many different laws," Slit Eyes finally said, "The law of the jungle, the law of the police and then my law—which, unfortunately, you did break."

"I don't see how that's possible since I've never met you before."

"If you keep repeating that you're going to start believing it. No, you broke the law all right. You broke the territorial law, the oldest law there is."

Kane's eyes fluttered excitedly just before he readjusted his glasses.

"This territory doesn't belong to you," Slit Eyes continued, "yet, I've watched you walk up and down it for hours as if you owned it. What are you doing all this time, anyway? I know you never actually get on a plane."

"I'm not doing anything."

"That's hard to believe, buddy. I mean you don't come here to look at all the travelers, just certain ones you want something from, am I right?"

"Nope, nothing," he finally said, suddenly realizing that Slit Eyes was substantially larger than him. "This is just a mistake."

"The only mistake is the one you're making setting up in my territory, you hear me?"

Kane suddenly thought it was drug dealing or maybe some kind of prostitution ring and rose from his seat. "I don't want any trouble," he said.

"No, I bet you don't, so sit down please."

Then Slit Eyes took out his cell phone and made a call. "He's at the bar," was all he said. In a matter of seconds, another man appeared before him, oddly stiff, as if he were made of porcelain, who was apparently going to escort him out of the airport.

"Let's go now," he said.

Kane followed him in silence, but as soon as they were out of Slit Eyes' sight, he began appealing to the escort.

"Don't worry; I'm leaving," Kane said to the escort. "I understand, I mean, I don't understand but I'm leaving, anyway. You think I'm doing something wrong, so..."

"My instructions are to accompany you out of the airport."

"Ok, but I'm leaving anyway. I was already leaving when you arrived."

"Maybe in your mind but your body was still in Terminal C."

"But, don't you see this isn't necessary? That I was already trying to leave when you arrived?"

"I'm just following my orders, sir."

They walked in silence for the next minute or two. The escort was about his height though, in all probability, considerably stronger and certainly was at least ten to fifteen years younger. He was wearing an old, tight-fitting, brown-leather jacket and wire-rimmed glasses. Suddenly, Kane felt a new anxiety.

"So does this mean that I can never return to the airport or just not to Terminal C?"

"Whatever you were told is what you should do."

Words to live by, Kane thought. Unfortunately, he was too upset to remember exactly what he was told.

"But that's just it, if I'd had a little more time, I could have explained that I wasn't spying or doing anything wrong, that I just sometimes hang out at airports to watch the planes take off. If I had a little more time, I could have explained all that."

"We'd all like a little more time."

"But can't I explain it to you? Can you listen to me now?"

The escort looked concerned and for the first time, turned his head toward Kane. "What would that accomplish?"

"Maybe if you listen to me and believe me, you could tell your boss he made a mistake."

The escort kept walking, looking straight ahead like a soldier.

"I'm not in a position where I can make promises," he said.

Kane felt a flicker of hope but instinctively also felt he shouldn't begin talking until they were out of the airport. The escort was acting in a very professional manner, after all, and might well loosen up and give him a minute or two once his task had been completed. They were headed towards the baggage terminal and ground transportation now. Kane wondered if the escort was armed and, if so, where he was concealing his weapon. Then he began rehearsing, in his mind, the way he could explain the attraction airports had for him. He decided he would describe it as the hobby of a lonely, recently retired man with no children (though he often fantasized about having them) that slowly became a constant activity. And was that really so unusual? Wasn't that essentially what happened to millions of people who repeatedly went to the movies or horse races or to public speeches? It wasn't so uncommon for a hobby to end up playing a major role in one's life. The only difference, in his case, was that there was no specific activity he came to see like the take-off of the planes—though he always relished seeing that. It was the random, unforeseen events of the airport, particularly at Terminal C, that were often the most fulfilling. The woman trying to calm down her toddler, the young couple unabashedly making out, the old man muttering to himself were all somehow fascinating to see, like animals in a zoo. But who could understand that?

They reached the streets and the deep-blue November sky. He was not prepared to face his empty apartment yet, where the picture of an airport scotch taped to the mirror above his bureau was the only thing he liked looking at.

"So are you done with your job now?"

"With you and for the rest of the night, too."

"Could I please talk with you then for just a minute?" he said, managing to finally make eye contact with the escort.

"There's nothing to be gained by that. Your dealings with us are over."

"Please, you have intelligent eyes," Kane blurted. (He was originally going to tell the escort that he had a kind face but thought that might be too threatening and also an atrocious cliché.)

The escort smiled. "I don't use it any place else so maybe all my intelligence gathered there."

"Let me buy you a drink," Kane said.

"There's no place to drink around here. I'm afraid there's nothing but taxis."

"Well, do you believe me that I was doing nothing wrong? That I wasn't even aware of the presence of your organization much less know what it's doing?"

"Who says there's an organization?"

"Whatever it is or isn't, I had nothing to do with it. I know nothing about it. Nothing. Do you believe me?"

"It's not important what I believe."

"It is to me," Kane said, with more passion than he'd intended. For the second time, he was able to sustain something like eye contact with the escort. "I think you do believe me, but why don't they?"

A look of surprise registered in the escort's bluish-black eyes. "They have to be careful—they have to err of the side of caution."

Kane nodded, feeling slightly dizzy. "Are you sure there's no place where I can buy you a drink?"

The escort looked around himself uneasily.

"We could talk right here for a few minutes. It's not too cold out, is it?"

"I guess not."

"But no questions about who I work for or what they're doing...okay?"

"Yes, I understand. I appreciate it. I certainly don't want to get you in trouble."

"I won't get in trouble as long as you stay out of the airport."

"But I thought it was just Terminal C I was supposed to stay away from?"

"I think the consensus is that if you come back to the airport, you won't be able to resist Terminal C."

"But I don't even know what you're doing there," Kane said.

"I'm afraid the consensus is that you already know too much. That's all I'm going to say."

"You know, I happen to be a very liberal fellow. So, even if I sensed something illegal going on—which I didn't—I wouldn't care. I'm very laissez-faire about drugs or prostitutes and personal rights."

"Drugs and prostitutes? Who said anything about that? Are you saying something?"

"No, not at all. I was just giving an example to show my live and let live attitude, that's all."

"Kind of a funny thing to talk about in terms of the airport, isn't it?"

Kane shrugged, "I've never been good at saying the right thing."

"Cause, if you wanted a hooker, why would you go to the airport? The two don't go together. It's like oil and water, right?"

"Of course, you're right. That's why I said I didn't mean anything by it."

But now that he was forced to think about it, he had noticed some oddly dressed children talking with people who seemed the wrong age to be their parents, and once, a few weeks ago, a boy had asked him what time it was in a strange way that sounded like "do you have any time?"

"'Course if you needed a woman I understand. Everyone gets lonely, right?"

"Yes," Kane said, thinking *especially me since I retired*, though he'd always thought he'd hated his job and would be immensely relieved when it ended.

"You know, I like you, in spite of tonight's unpleasant events."

"Misunderstanding, I'd call it."

"Yeah, sure. The point is I might be able to help you meet a woman who'd be right for you. It is women you're interested in, right?"

"Yes," Kane said, though he couldn't

remember the last time he'd thought of one in a sexual way.

"Grown women?"

"Of course," Kane said.

"Follow me, then."

"Where are we going?"

"To my car. You have a credit card, don't you?"

"Yes."

"And you know enough not to mention this to anyone, right?"

"I know."

"Follow me."

He wanted to go home, yet he didn't. Wanted to lie down in his own bed and rest his legs and look at his pictures of airplanes and yet didn't want to be alone in such a quiet, closed-in space that he sometimes thought of as a crypt. In a way, he felt grateful to the escort for deciding for him, though he didn't know what to make of the dark-haired, heavy-set woman sitting opposite him now in the small South City bar who seemed to be forcing out gap-toothed smiles like a candy dispenser. Was she really working for the escort? It was certainly not unbelievable that the escort had a side business apart from the airport, but it was unusual to pimp a woman who was at least 50 and probably, once the make-up was scraped off, more like 55. Still, to Kane, she looked more than young enough.

"You new in town?" she said.

Kane stared at her blindingly red lips.

"No, I've been in the city almost my whole life."

"Really?" she said, absently, with barely the energy to ask another question. He felt she'd already lost all interest in him, if, indeed, she'd ever had any.

"My name's Georgette but people call me Georgy."

Kane nodded and sipped at his whisky sour. He was thinking, so many days nothing happens and then suddenly everything happens at once so you're always unprepared. Nevertheless, he managed to make passable conversation with her for the next few minutes. She asked him about his job, and he told her that he'd worked in an office but was now retired.

"What's it like to be retired?" she said, forcing out another smile.

"It's been kind of a quiet challenge," he said, with an ironic smile of his own.

"What do you mean?" she said, looking at him with what appeared to be genuine interest all of a sudden.

"How to fill up your time. It gets a little lonely sometimes."

"I hear you," Georgy said, apparently to show empathy. "Do you have any family?"

He told her he was an only child and an orphan.

"I'm sorry," she said. He then explained that he'd never felt close with his parents who were somewhat disengaged with him—preoccupied with their work and troubles.

"My parents passed, too," she said. "I guess I'm lucky to have Ari."

"Who's Ari?" Kane said, unable to camouflage a tinge of jealousy.

"Oh, I thought you knew him. He's the man who introduced us," she said, finishing her drink.

"Oh," Kane said, with obvious disappointment.

"So, he's a close friend of yours?" He was trying to picture again how exactly the escort looked.

"He's my brother," Georgy blurted, "but I

wasn't supposed to tell you that. Are you good at keeping secrets?"

"My whole life is a secret, even to me."

"What do you mean? Are you some kind of spy or something?"

Again, he was being asked the same thing that Slit Eyes wanted to know—immediately he told her no. Was she possibly working for the organization, trying through a different way to find out what he was really doing in Terminal C?

Georgy looked at him meaningfully, "What do you say we continue this conversation upstairs in my room?"

"Okay," Kane said, "I didn't know there were rooms above this place."

It was impossible that he was in this under-lit room with Georgy, yet here he was. Just as it was impossible that he was forced out of Terminal C by Georgy's brother. It was an inconceivable night, yet even such nights had their limits. Georgy was already in her underwear, her large, sagging breasts more than half exposed.

"You know, I don't really think I can, you know, do anything tonight."

"What?" she said, her big brown eyes opening up to an almost comic degree. "You ain't tried me yet, so how can you know?"

"You're very attractive, of course, and very nice, but my arthritis is acting up and my legs hurt pretty bad and I have other physical problems, too."

"You want me to just suck your dick?"

"No, no, even that would be difficult. I'm sorry," he added, "believe me, I'd like to."

"You already paid my brother, right?"

"Yes."

"'Cause you can't get your money back."

"Of course, I understand. I enjoyed talking to you a lot. Actually, I'm wondering if you could possibly tell me a good place where I could get a taxi home?"

"Taxi? Taxis don't come down here. You probably have to walk five blocks to get one. You walk five blocks south, you might have a chance."

Kane felt his heart beat. He didn't want to walk in this neighborhood at night.

"You look kinda worried."

Kane shrugged without looking at her. "It's just been a long day," he finally managed.

"'Course I could give you a ride if you wanted to wait 'til morning."

Kane looked at the bed, knowing he wouldn't be able to sleep for a minute. Still, it seemed the better choice.

"You'd give me a ride? Or charge me for one?"

"Give you one in the morning. I'm too tired now."

"That's very kind of you."

"Yeah, you finally met the hooker with the heart of gold," she said, laughing.

He forced a laugh, wondering what the two of them would talk about and hoping her idea of morning was before noon, which would still be ten hours away, and yet there was nothing he was really looking forward to doing in his apartment now.

She'd begun talking about herself and then she'd begun drinking again. She'd asked him to drink, too, but he steadfastly declined. He was afraid of how alcohol might make him feel, though he didn't tell that to Georgy.

They were sitting in her small living room

at what looked like a card table where she was drinking vodka tonic. Every now and then he looked at the window where a street lamp shaped like a dinosaur seemed to be peering at them.

"So, I suppose a well-mannered man like you is wondering how I got into this line of work."

Kane shrugged. "No, I really wasn't."

"Ain't much to tell, anyway. Ari and me never had much money."

"You do what you have to do to get by," Kane said.

"Look at what Ari does."

Kane looked at her intensely, as if her face would tell him what it was. "How do you mean?"

"Taking people out of the airport who look too nosey or threatening. Humiliating them that way."

"So, he doesn't like doing it, then?"

"'Course not. Who would? Taking people out into the night and leaving them alone. They all tell him they're innocent, too, he told me, and half of them probably are."

"I was innocent." Kane said.

"I'm sure you were, most of 'em are completely innocent. Ari knows that. If he thought there was something wrong with you, he wouldn't have brought you to me."

"And what about what they're doing—the people who ordered Ari to throw me out."

"What do you mean?"

"Is what they're doing innocent, too?"

She finished her drink and said, "Don't ask me that. That's a professional secret."

"A professional secret," Kane repeated with more than a trace of sarcasm. "Is it different than a personal secret or just a regular secret?"

"You know what I mean. I talk too much when I drink."

"Sometimes, I think there should be a

museum of secrets to show all the secrets man has tried to keep through the ages, most of which eventually get found out. You know I had a philosophy professor in college who once said in class, 'the secrets of man are so trivial they're hardly worth mentioning'—get it?"

"Yeah, you could look at it that way. And by the way, I'm really impressed that you went to college. I didn't know that I had such an intellectual client on my hands."

Kane blushed, fearing he had somehow been immodest.

"Anyway, some secrets never get found out," Georgy said.

"Like what?"

"Like who killed JFK."

"That kind of got found out but granted..."

"And who killed Jon Benet. You can't deny that one."

"There's not much doubt in my mind about that one but you're right, from an objective point of view, that's a secret."

"See, I ain't so dumb after all seeing as I can keep up with a college man like you."

"I never meant to suggest otherwise. In fact, I'm sure you know dozens and dozens of secrets, just about Terminal C alone, don't you?"

"Yeah, but you'll never get me to tell you any, so quit trying. You already agreed to that."

Kane sighed. "You're right, I did promise. In the grand scheme of things, what goes on in Terminal C is probably pretty trivial anyway. We only focus on the little secrets 'cause we'll never know the big ones like why was the world made and, even more interesting, how. I mean, how could there always have been something, but how could there ever have been nothing?"

"You think about stuff like that, you'll drive yourself ape shit."

Kane laughed, "You've got a point there."

He always knew she wanted to talk—why else would she ask him to stay the night? But around three AM, he began to realize that the talking was going to last all night. He could only hope that when it got light out and before she'd go to sleep, he'd get his ride home that she'd promised. Meanwhile, his legs were starting to ache again, which caused him to shift uncomfortably in his chair. Every now and then he heard shouting or laughter from the bar below.

It was a strange story she told him—parts of it were interesting, if he regarded them as individual scenes in a play, but he often couldn't see how these parts related to each other or what the overarching theme of the play was. (There was something he admired about airports—they had a clear purpose—to travel from one place to another, of course, and everything else, like the restaurants and newsstands and gift shops, was related to that central purpose.) He felt a little pain in his heart as he thought of Terminal C, where its ostensible order had been violated by some secret organization, no doubt up to no good.

Georgy was talking about her mother again, who was also a hooker.

"We didn't have much," Georgy said, "but she always kept clothes on my back and food in my stomach. Well, you can see I do very good at keeping food in my stomach."

Kane looked puzzled.

"Meaning, I'm a big woman who likes to eat, and drink, too, I admit. I guess we all pay the price for our appetites."

Kane thought wistfully of Terminal C again. How he'd miss eating at the Chili's there!

She finished another drink. She was drinking from a bottle of cheap, red wine now, and after she placed the bottle down, their eyes met for a moment, which seemed to prompt her to start a different story.

"Sometimes, when I'm in between customers it gets kind of quiet and spooky here..."

"Spooky?" Kane said.

"Yeah, like overly quiet so all's you hear are your thoughts, and you get kind of lonely and end up doing some strange things to distract yourself from your thoughts."

"What strange things?"

"I noticed you looking at my hands."

Had he been? He wasn't aware of it, but all these Terminal C people—Terminal C terminators really—were always accusing him of doing things he'd never done.

"I wasn't looking at your hands," he finally managed.

"Well, I thought you were, and I'm sure you saw something funny."

Kane shrugged, suddenly afraid to speak.

"Want to know a secret? I did that, mostly, to myself."

"To yourself?"

"Oh, yeah, I told you I was different. But I don't do it as much now. Maybe I shouldn't have told you that. Ari told me never to tell anybody. But what the hell are secrets, like you said."

"Doesn't it hurt?"

"You'd think so but you get used to it and it gives you something to do—puts you in another world if it's done right. I used to let my customers do it to me but then some of them would get carried away and cut me too deep and sometimes try knives on me. You don't look like you'd ever do a thing like that," she said, looking at him closely, "if I ever was to ask you."

Kane stared at her and felt his heart beat. Despite his weak legs, he got to his feet in a start.

"I couldn't do anything like that. I'm sorry," he added, being sure to avoid the disappointed look in her eyes. "I'd better be going now," Kane said, knowing he would have to face the silent, cold streets alone as he waited and hoped for a cab. They weren't scheduled with departures and arrival times like planes. They appeared and left mysteriously and were more like people that way.

He took his coat from her small, pink sofa and put it on rapidly despite the arthritis he had in his left shoulder.

"Guess I freaked you out about my habit."

Kane shrugged.

"I was doing fine till then," she added. "Well, it's an old story, me and my big mouth. Here I thought we was becoming friends and then I opened my mouth and ruined it."

Kane was stunned by her words and looked at her closely as she rose from the table, looking young enough to be his daughter. He heard a noise then, perhaps from the bar, perhaps from the sky—if planes were still taking off at this hour.

"We could be platonic friends," he said. It would probably be just once or twice, like when he was a kid flying kites a couple of times with his father in the neighborhood park. His father had talked about taking him to the White Mountains in New Hampshire. They never went but it was still fun to think about.

Meanwhile, Georgy was looking at him closely. "Here, take my card so you can call me on my private cell."

His hand trembled a little as he took it. "Thank you," he said, wondering how long he should wait till he could call her. Then he turned to leave.

"Well, goodbye and thanks again."

"Wait," she said, "You forgot I'm driving you home now."

Kane smiled broadly as he watched her put on her coat quickly too, even though it seemed too small for her. It was a dark winter coat and, at first, seemed almost as dark as her hair. But when he looked more closely, he saw it was really a deep shade of blue like the sky. Then he noticed a faux fur collar that made the coat look oddly alive. It was funny what a coat could do.

COLD OCEAN

He was in search of strange sights or not so much strange sights as new ones. His mother had died just over three months ago, and even though the illness leading up to it was fairly long, he was still shocked, as if his brain couldn't quite adapt.

There weren't many people he could talk to about this, (there were always only a few people he could talk to) in this case only one. He was a man a little older than himself named Harvey, who worked in a bookstore in the Village, who he sometimes had a drink or dinner with after Harvey got out of work. He listened to Harvey only because his mother had died, too. It was Harvey who suggested he go someplace new for a few days, to a place that wasn't "saturated with memories of your mother" as he put it. Harvey said he had gone to Utah and then to Santa Fe after his mother died and claimed that it helped. "It's not as if your grief will disappear, Barry, but it will do some good."

"I don't want to go far," Barry said. "It would be too hard."

Harvey nodded. He was the sympathetic type. They were eating quietly at a Japanese restaurant in the Village. There was one other quality of Harvey's he especially admired—his superior sense of geography. It was as if while he spoke about a place, he was looking at it on a very reliable map. It was like that at the Japanese restaurant too, as if he'd placed an elaborate map of the United States on the table cloth that not only had all the states in their correct positions but how long it would take to get to each one from New York.

"There's a two-step process of elimination we need to follow," Harvey said, tugging at his beard that was prematurely gray. "First, we need to select a place that isn't too far away. Second, it needs to be a place you haven't been to with your mother."

Barry had told Harvey about all the trips he'd taken with his mother after she got her money, money that was now his. He'd told Harvey about his missing father as well. He'd told Harvey quite a lot but he'd also kept a lot hidden.

"I think we need to add a third condition," Harvey said. "I think it needs to be a place that's not only new and not too far away but also one that has impact. A place with some real impact sights."

A number of places were proposed and eliminated: New Orleans, Kansas City, and the outer banks in North Carolina. Finally Harvey brought up Chicago. He spoke of it with great enthusiasm and precision as if he were making a presentation at a conference. Barry was unmoved until he began to describe the beach. "It's in the middle of the city and it's startling, surrealistic, like seeing the sand and ocean in the middle of Fifth Avenue."

There's no ocean in Chicago, Barry pointed out, but Harvey said Lake Michigan was so big it looked just like the ocean. "Wait till you see the beach surrounded by the tallest buildings of the city, I swear you've never seen anything like it."

...It was the beach Barry was on now. Oddly, there weren't many people there though it was a close to perfect beach day in early June. The sky was a pure light blue with the last little wisps of cloud lifting above the Hancock Observatory and the other huge buildings in the distance looming over the beach like a pack of dinosaurs, just like Harvey said.

A lifeguard directed him to a men's room in a tunnel at the far edge of the beach, and he changed into his suit there. He thought of how much his mother would have loved it here, how happy the two of them could have been and he nearly doubled over in pain. But she'd have wanted him to be happy, wouldn't she, he thought, as he ran out of the vast tunnel.

He was carrying his clothes in one of his traveling bags and was wearing the white towel he took from the hotel over his shoulder. The towel was as white as the few slowly sailing bits of cloud. His bathing suit was as black as his hair–he was glad Harvey talked him into buying it just before his trip. Lake Michigan, however, was a sharper shade of blue than the sky, but all the colors of the day were clear and distinct. That was his last thought before he went in the water. After he swam for a while he was glad he picked Chicago for his trip. He was beginning to relax a little, and he needed to relax and plot his next move, though with his inheritance he had enough money so he wouldn't have to work for at least five years (some said ten) and if he invested it well, maybe not ever. Still, Barry thought he should probably do something, just in case his novel didn't work out, which he hadn't begun to actually write down yet.

...When he first saw her walking towards him she was wearing dark sunglasses so he couldn't tell if she meant to talk to him or not. It was just a body in a one-piece, white bathing suit and a pair of sunglasses. It was a good body, too, and it moved well. He'd just come in from the water and was toweling off.

"Hi there," she said in a Midwestern friendly voice. "How's the water?"

"Great," he said, "cold but great. You should go in."

"I've been in already. I was in this morning."

"Really?"

"Now that's when the water was really cold."

Barry laughed. For some reason he wanted to please this woman, in part because her body was good (nice cleavage, shapely breasts and legs, although her thighs looked a little slack and fleshy) but also because she seemed so innocent and friendly standing there in front of him in her white suit. He thought Harvey would approve.

"Do you come here a lot?" he asked, shifting his weight so that one foot dug in a little deeper in the sand.

"Almost every day. I guess I'm a real beach bum."

He looked at her face and especially her neck to try to figure out how old she was. He wished she would take her sunglasses off, but since she was keeping them on, he concentrated on her neck because he'd read somewhere that that was the best indicator of age, the hardest place to camouflage.

"Are you from here originally?" Barry said, continuing to interview her.

"Yeah, I'm a Chicago girl. I was out in the suburbs in Winnetka for a time and then I taught for a while in Santa Barbara."

"Santa Barbara," he said, thinking of his mother and the times they'd been there.

"Santa Barbara is beautiful."

"It sure is. But you know what, it's beautiful here, too."

"Oh, of course. What were you teaching?"

She told him but it didn't make sense. It was some subject in which the words "communication" and "ontology" both occurred. Then, suddenly, she took off her sunglasses and extended her hand.

"I'm Marianne Brodney," she said, with the same guileless smile on her face.

He smiled, too, as he shook hands with her. She was definitely older than he thought. Her face had aged more than her body, although it was a pleasant face with gray-blue eyes. Her hair, which was almost certainly dyed, was a mix of blond and gray and a little on the thin side.

"I'm Bill, Bill Gordon," he said, giving her a fake name without exactly knowing why. He was thinking now that she might be anywhere from 45 to her early 50's, but he tried not to stare too hard at her. He asked her when she was in Santa Barbara to see if their time there had overlapped.

"Let's see," she said, "I'm 56 now and I was 35 then, so it must have been in 1982."

He told her he was there the year before or maybe the year after. He was thinking that she was even older than his mother would have been but there she was with her hand on her hip, apparently flirting with him, although with these friendly Midwesterners it was sometimes hard to tell. She continued talking affably about her experiences teaching in a community college in Long Island. There wasn't a trace of self-consciousness in her. Everything was said in a straightforward way, although when she told him her age there was more than a little trace of pride in her voice.

He had to admit he wasn't listening very carefully to what she was saying. The shock of her age and the way she was now clearly flirting with him and then, of course, the issue of what he was going to do about it, were preoccupying him.

"How long are you in town for?" she asked.

"A few days, probably," he said, seeing a brief look of disappointment on her face. "Maybe more. I'm playing it by ear."

"That's a good way to play things."

"It's always been my way," he said, pleased with the way that sounded.

"Mine too, when I have the guts to do it," she said laughing. "Is this your first time in Chicago?"

"Actually, it is. I've traveled quite a bit, but for some reason I never got around to coming here."

"Is that a slight east coast accent I detect?"

"From Boston originally," he said. He always said Boston, never Brookline, the town next to it where he was really born.

"So, are you here on business, pleasure or some combination?"

He knew where this was going. She wanted to know what his job was just as if she were researching him as a potential date on the Internet.

"Strictly for pleasure. I'm fortunately in a financial position where I don't have to work, at least not at any kind of job. I'm a writer."

"Really?" she said, not as if she doubted him, but as if he impressed her. He felt the first stirrings of an erection, nothing overwhelming, but pleasant nonetheless.

"What kind of writing do you do?"

"I'm a novelist and film script writer, and I also write some on the philosophy of aesthetics."

She made a sound to show she was impressed.

He wondered if he should have added the last part. She was an academic and might know about Aesthetics. But he did, too, a little. He had to remind himself it was just that he didn't have the degree— and what did degrees have to do with knowledge? Nothing, nada. Had there ever been a professor that he couldn't keep up with who didn't assume that he was a professor himself, as well as a well-published author? Degrees meant nothing; book contracts meant nothing either as far as the quality of one's work was concerned. He, of all people, should know that, he reminded himself. Degrees and book contracts were parts of the same disease, the same self-validation complex that obsessed America. Why did he even bother to debate this in his mind any longer with one foot now dug in fairly firmly in the sand as he faced this 56-year-old freak of nature with her 35-year-old body, stretching and putting her hand on her hip, patting herself constantly in different places, like a used car salesman showing off his latest car.

She was asking him if he had taught anywhere.

"Mostly in France and a little bit in New York. I actually prefer not to teach unless it's a special situation. Not that I don't have great respect for teachers and the profession, I do," he added quickly after seeing that fleeting look of disappointment pass over her again. "It's just that my writing projects have become increasingly demanding and time consuming."

"Wow, that's really exciting. Where can I get one of your books?"

"I'll send you one."

"Oh no..."

"But of course I will. You just have to give me your address, that's all."

"Okay. Well that's exciting. I'll give you my address, and you'll lend me one of your books."

"I'll give you one of my books."

"That's really generous of you," she said. She seemed to mean it, and he felt his erection stiffen another notch. She stopped talking then. It was like a fish coming up for air for a second, and he stood there without saying anything either. Then she asked him if he wanted to go in the water with her, something that he once again hadn't foreseen. Barry looked at the lake— the water was difficult for him because he and his mother had always taken vacations near the water except for their time in Paris together. Even then they'd taken a trip to the South of France and went swimming there.

"I don't know, it's pretty cold."

"Come on," she said, grabbing his hand for a second, "it will be fun."

She let go of his hand then and ran into the water. He watched her from behind. Then he ran in after her and soon was swimming next to her. They were both laughing and talking louder than they needed to. There were only two or three other people in the water yet Marianne and he were talking as if airplanes were roaring overhead. For a few seconds they even splashed each other. She splashed him first (which was surprising) and he splashed her back.

When they separated for a while he sensed that she wanted him to watch her swim so he did. As he suspected, she was very athletic. She was a better swimmer than him. It made him smile but feel strangely challenged at the same time, even angry. It was somewhat disturbing, and he headed back to shore.

They both talked about how great it felt after they came in from the water, but they stood apart from each other while they toweled off. She started chattering again. For the first time he felt she might be slightly nervous. She was making a laundry list of places he had to go to in Chicago before he left. The Art Institute, of course; and The Field Museum and also the Aquarium and Buckingham Fountain and The Hancock Observatory, which had a better view of the city than the Sears Tower, though the Sears Tower was taller; and The Jazz Record Mart, which had one of the best jazz collections in the world and The Art Museum and then there was always The White Sox and The Cubs.

"Do you like baseball?" she asked.

"Sure."

She looked straight at him for a few seconds, then down at her pocketbook she was holding. "I'm looking for a piece of paper and a pen so I can give you my address," she said, "and I can't seem to find either."

"Do you live in an apartment or..."

"I live in a condominium, just three blocks away."

"A condominium on Lake Shore Drive. Not bad."

"Near Lake Shore Drive, not exactly on it. But it's only about three blocks away."

"Still not bad. How about when you're ready to leave, I'll walk you home, and then I'll see where you live and get your address that way?"

This time she looked surprised.

"That's a good idea," she said, "let's do it."

He smiled, too. He was impressed at how bold he was being and felt pleased with himself again. "If you have some kind of doorman I could even get it on paper."

"I'm sure we can manage that," she said smiling.

It was kind of exciting in a way to think of a 56-year-old woman going down to the beach trying to pick up younger men, as he imagined she did, men young enough to be her sons.

Testing her mettle every day on the beach with her body— was it still good enough to attract the young ones and then, later, was it good enough to satisfy them?

Ten or fifteen minutes later, he decided to leave the beach, and he went back to the tunnel to change into his clothes.

"Here's your last chance to leave," Barry said, laughing, although he didn't think he'd said it loud enough for her to hear. He didn't know what he wanted to do—he had contradictory impulses, which were upsetting him so he was surprised that while he was changing he was actually hurrying as if he really was afraid she'd leave. When he finally finished and left the tunnel, he looked out and waved at her and she immediately waved back. Strange, he thought, the little dance of manners that preceded sex, especially sex with someone for the first time, as if people had to reassure themselves that even at their most animalistic they retained their essential human identity.

He began walking next to her, she in her white terry cloth robe, he back in his green shirt and black pants. She continued to supply the conversation in her even keeled way although it was more sporadic now and more quiet.

"There's my building," she said, pointing to it when they were less than a block away.

"Very spiffy," he said. He considered himself a quick study and was now pretty good at Midwestern affability himself. He decided he wouldn't say no to her but that she would have to make the first move. There was a small possibility that he'd misread the situation, and he didn't want to embarrass himself, not in the fragile state he was in.

"Would you like to see it?" she said, looking directly at him with only a trace of a smile.

"Sure, I'd like that." He passed the doorman, a guy about his age in an uncomfortable looking uniform. He wondered how many times he'd seen men going upstairs with Marianne before and even looked to the doorman's face as if for an answer, though it gave away nothing.

In the elevator they stood a polite distance apart.

"I live on the top floor," she said, with an expression that was part proud, part embarrassed, as if she knew he was wondering how a divorced teacher could afford such a place.

Barry nodded to show he was impressed, and when he first saw her condo, white and airy and spacious with a panoramic view from her picture window of Lake Michigan and the very beach he'd been on a few minutes ago, he said, "It's beautiful." She put her pocket book on a glass table in the living room. She had a lot of glass furniture. He considered making a joke about The Glass Menagerie but thought better of it. Instead he pointed to a dark wooden sculpture that looked to be African and asked her about it.

"Don't you love it? I got that on a trip to Kenya. I had a wonderful time in Africa, went on a safari, went in the jungle, did everything, the works."

"I'm coming to the conclusion that I'm very lucky to have met you in Chicago since you travel more than anyone I know."

"Really? I feel like I'm home a lot. Anyway, I've never lived in any place as glamorous as you when you were in Paris all those years. And all the famous people you met— Gore Vidal, Susan Sontag and Beckett, didn't you say Beckett?"

"Yes. I knew him when I was very young."

"God, what was he like? I used to teach 'Godot' to my students in Winnetka."

"Beckett is...sui generis," he said with a

strong but not overly grand gesture, hoping the phrase and the gesture would put a halt to too many more questions about Beckett whom he'd never met. Though he could have, he thought; he should have. He knew someone in Paris who had met him. Actually he should have had a father like Beckett, someone wise and ethical and brilliant and...sui generis. He would have known how to handle his mother, known how to give him some space from her when she got hysterical and was all over him, which was at least half the time.

"That's the difference between you and me," Marianne was saying with a smile. "I teach the writers to my class and you know them and are one yourself."

He laughed along with her. They were standing at opposite sides of the living room. He beside the wooden sculpture and the glass table and she in front of the large pink sofa underneath her picture window.

He moved a few steps closer, and she said, "Do you think it's too early in the day for a drink?"

"Not for me it isn't," he said, and she laughed as if he'd said something exceedingly witty.

"I'll go get them," she said, still smiling at him, not quite blushing, but something close to it. She promptly walked into the kitchen and returned with a bottle of champagne and two glasses. She set everything down on the low rectangular glass table in front of the pink sofa.

"Would you like to open?" she said, gesturing towards him with the bottle and opener in her hand.

"I'm afraid I'm completely inept at that. You'll have a much better chance of success if you do it."

She smiled—she was amenable to everything. He liked that. He thought one glass might be enough. She poured well, too; just a little overflowed.

"To us," she said, as their glasses clinked.

"Gee, champagne. I feel like a king," he said, as they both put down their glasses.

"You are a king to me."

Their hands touched. He was feeling strangely happy, like his soul was made of champagne. He reached back for his glass and swallowed the rest of it.

He sensed that she felt comfortable with everything, too. She'd told him her age, or something close to it, and about her divorce (her husband had stopped being interested in her, which Barry translated as he stopped having sex with her) and about her travels and her life of teaching school— he could tell she was one of those devoted type school teachers. She'd been so candid about everything and obviously felt very good about it. She exuded self-respect and merely hoped he liked what she said.

"No reason to let the rest of the bottle go to waste," she said, pouring them both another glass.

"No reason at all," he said, laughing.

So she wanted a little help, she wasn't quite as sturdy as she appeared, or else she just liked getting high. Either way, he liked it. As soon as he finished the next glass, his hands went straight to her breasts, and she put up no resistance at all. She moaned a little and said, "that feels nice."

When he went to unhook her bra, he thought she'd help him right away but she didn't. She was old school. She gave him a shot at doing it first, and eventually he succeeded. They were good-sized breasts, too, quite firm for her age. She was proud of them and deserved to be. He kissed her and she kissed him back, a little too eagerly for his taste, making him think briefly of a squirrel chewing a nut. The next ones were better, though. His hand went down and locked with hers, and they walked to her room.

Her bedroom was like a continuation of her living room, as if it were the living room's daughter. There was a wall-length picture window looking out over Chicago. In the distance he could see the blue of the lake. There were glass tables and a thick, off-white carpet on the floor. The only other color in the room was her pink bedspread. He expected to see some photographs of her family, then remembered that she'd said she had no children.

He lay down on the bed and kissed her but kept his eyes open. She had a kind of self-satisfied smile on her face, which he found exciting but also aggravating, almost as if she was having an adventure at his expense. He shut his eyes and tried not to think about it. Soon he began to enjoy himself again and even wished she lived near him in New York. Not too near in the city but maybe somewhere in a suburb. It would help him during this time when he was trying to get over his mother, which was like trying to forget about the sun or the ocean—impossible, of course.

"I wish you lived in New York, near me," he said.

"I'm here now, let's enjoy our now together."

Her remark, so typical, like something smuggled out of EST or Zen Buddism for Midwesterners, irritated him. He slid down on the bed and decided to concentrate on pleasing her so he wouldn't have to think of her or his mother either.

That worked out well, and for a while made things better. It was comforting in a way and oddly enjoyable, too, as he braced himself for her moment of release. But it didn't happen. Soon he began to feel as if he were in a tunnel whose walls were slowly closing in. He wanted to get out, afraid that he wouldn't be able to breathe but he stayed on task, imagining he was in a medical situation where he had to do this to save her life. Finally her muscles started to contract, like a twitching fish in the ocean, and she moaned and it was over.

He let her rest for a while before he penetrated her. But almost as soon as he began, he was staggered by images of his mother. There were even pictures of her on the beach with him—the beach a combination of one in Cape Cod and one in Santa Barbara that he'd been to with her. Those were beaches where he'd laughed and held her hand, when the two of them were away at last from everything that could ruin it, in a place where they'd embraced and she'd looked at him with real love in her eyes while she said, "Barry, my beautiful son."

To distract himself from these memories, he had to do it hard, but Marianne didn't say anything and squeezed his hand when it was over.

Now he was alone, as if on an island far out in the ocean. He might have stayed there, but he had just enough social conditioning, he figured, to lie down beside her, even to look at her face. He wasn't surprised to see her smiling as if to say, "I won." She'd gotten her orgasm the way she wanted without even having to ask for it and then withstood his strongest thrusts without even once asking him to ease up a bit.

There was no question it was a smile of tremendous self-satisfaction. A smile that exuded pride in her body, which was good enough to attract a man young enough to be her son and strong enough to not be hurt by him either. Pride also in so effortlessly pulling the whole thing off that began with the easy way she approached him on the beach to its ending just a minute ago.

Like her body in general, the smile had extraordinary staying power. He found that he couldn't stop looking at it. It was both repulsive and fascinating as if a beautiful spider, mounted on some kind of platform, had joined the two of them in bed. Finally, he had to close his eyes because he couldn't stand to see that spider smile anymore so he pretended that he needed to rest (which must have made her feel still stronger) even at the risk of seeing his mother again once he closed his eyes.

He didn't look at Marianne but he talked with her a little longer, etiquette too, of course, socialization—as strong a force as Niagara Falls. It went all right at first until she said "What a nice day this has been." It was her way of complimenting him without making herself too vulnerable—he knew all that—expressing her pleasure without directly attributing it to him. Meanwhile he knew she hoped for something more definitive back from him and that made him angry though he didn't say anything about it and solved the immediate problem by simply agreeing with her. That's when he got the idea because he was still angry at her miserly compliment after all the time he spent on her—not to mention the reassurances and compliments he gave her earlier in the day about her job and condominium. Yet, she couldn't even bring herself to say that his mouth was wonderful, much less that he was. How could he defile the memory of his mother, who really loved him and told him so all the time, with the likes of this aging, narcissistic school teacher? How repellent she was in her smug self-satisfaction, this woman who had undeservedly lived longer than his mother and now was basking in the pleasure of having enjoyed her son.

These were the things he thought about while he pictured the layout of her living room like a photograph he couldn't stop looking at. It made it virtually impossible to talk.

"Are you tired? Would you like to take a nap?" she offered, realizing, of course, that he had stopped talking.

"Will you take a nap, too?" he forced himself to say.

"Sure," she said, giving his hand a little squeeze. "I can always sleep after making love." He felt another jolt of pain. He didn't like how she lumped him in with all her other lovers with whom she also liked to nap after they were through. Yes, there was even more reason to do it now.

He waited. It wasn't long. In less than five minutes she turned on her side, perhaps to stifle her snoring, and fell sound asleep.

He crept out of the bed as quietly as he could, stepping as lightly as possible with his bare toes on her carpet. He was grateful to the carpet and to her large, well-made bed that made a minimum of noise when he got up. Odd to be grateful to things, as if they had souls like people, he thought as he picked up his clothes. He carried them into the living room, thinking that he would change there.

But once in the living room, he decided to take one more precaution. He went back to her room and slowly closed the door. That way if she got up suddenly, he'd be warned and could even come up with a story of some sort.

He changed into his clothes in front of the picture window in her living room, then went directly to the circular glass table and looked inside of her pocketbook. In the middle of it was a wallet, fat and red, as he knew it would be. There was cash in it too, several hundred dollars at least, which he withdrew and put in his pockets. He didn't want to mess with her credit cards. That would be far too risky, and beside, he'd made his point. Next time when someone did yeoman's work on her she wouldn't be so stingy with her compliments. She'd learn it would be a lot less expensive that way.

The most dangerous part would be closing her door and leaving her apartment. He opened and shut the door in one continuous motion. It made very little noise. He walked down the hall to the elevator, pushed the elevator button and waited, wondering if he should run downstairs. A moment later he realized that she could call out to him and not hearing anything walk out into the hall and see him by the elevator. What would he say then? What could he say?

He began to run down the stairs then. It was like running down ice. He couldn't think— could only concentrate on moving as fast as possible as if he were a kind of giant centipede racing for its life.

There was no side exit that he could see. When he reached the lobby, he looked up and saw the doorman reading the sports page of the Chicago Tribune. The paper rustled while he looked at him. They exchanged nods and then he went out to the street. Once he turned the corner he felt her money in his pockets and began to run. He was scared but also strangely happy.

Harvey was right; I'll have to come to Chicago more often, he said to himself. It was one of the lines he'd said to her in bed that had made her laugh. He tried to laugh out loud then, to make audible the sound he heard in his head, but it sounded hollow and weirdly shriveled like a muffled cough.

Then he thought of his mother and wanted to

scream but didn't, instead dug his nails as hard as he could into the palms of his hands.

"But I did it to vindicate you," he said to her over and over. "Don't you know that? I vindicated you, didn't I?"

He shook his head and started running, wondering if the dead understood about vindication.

A LETTER IN LAS VEGAS

"Because their words had forked no lightning."
–Dylan Thomas

The letter he emailed to your hotel a few hours after your conversation lay on the bed beside you and just looking at the exclamation points that recurred fugue-like throughout it (a fugue you could also hear in your mind like drumbeats or thunder) made you resist reading it. But what other choice did you have? For nearly 48 hours the same hideous "horror movie" of two nights ago had been playing repeatedly in your mind, the "movie" that had made you call your brother and him write you in the first place. The only other option to escape it was the TV in your room, but it had just three unwatchable channels working so it wasn't really an option at all. You knew that Sid, at the front desk, who you'd paid to misinform your brother, wouldn't fix it. He'd already promised to send someone up twice, but no one had come.

You picked up the letter. It was odd—you avoided someone and then you found yourself scrutinizing his letter.

"Darren, I'm going to write you very candidly," it began. "There's no question of pride anymore as there often was between us—I'm far too scared for that! You need to come home now, you know that. If you don't, it would be the worst, most self-destructive thing you could do! You told me once that you sometimes think of me as the police you keep trying to outrun or outwit, as if my goal is to arrest you rather than just being with you. I say this now, and everything else, only because I want you to fight the mess you're in instead of running away from it. Remember, I've known you your whole life, and right now I may be the only person, besides you, who can help you!"

You looked away from the letter, staring straight ahead at the Venetian blinds. You were aware there was a fundamental conflict in the way you and David were thinking about your situation. To him it all boiled down to your getting out of Las Vegas immediately to have your operation and deal with your other medical problems at home in Philadelphia. But to you, the primary issue was how to get to the next moment without seeing the "horror movie" again, how to escape from it, if only for a few minutes. So far, the letter wasn't working very well, but you still returned to it, this time skipping ahead a little.

"'Sins are like snowflakes, no two are alike.' You once wrote that in a letter to me, your proud and slightly envious older brother, while you were still getting your MFA and I agreed and obviously remembered it. Are you sure your not returning my phone calls or emails I've been sending all day isn't your own special kind of sin, the sin of making me worry so much I'm on the verge of flying out to Vegas myself to try to find you? I wonder if you realize what I'm going through, especially when I remember all your dark, hysterical talk on the phone like 'Death is tucked into life like an invisible napkin' and 'I have a lifetime of regret without the lifetime to regret it,' (you see how I can quote you) among other cheerful thoughts. I think you were born spouting aphorisms. You should have lived in ancient Greece!"

You laughed. That was what you thought you needed to "feel" him again—that sarcastic humor of David's and the kind of passionate innocence that lay behind it. In feeling all that, you finally got relief from the horror movie so you went back to the letter once more.

"Before Las Vegas, I thought your life (and our relationship) was at least functional. More specifically you were already somewhat avoiding me but you were under a lot of pressure after the results of your biopsy and, of course, I was shocked too! Still my feeling, based on what you told me on the phone, was that you were in reasonable spirits about going to Vegas, even a bit excited since you'd never been there before. And why not? The university there was paying you well, you'd already been interviewed and had your book praised by the city's best known alternative paper and you were even going to have your reading televised by a local cable TV show! And your reading was from any objective point of view a success and was received with warm, spontaneous applause. It was a kind of grand slam—like winning all the literary slots. Also, Bennet, your host from the English department there couldn't have been nicer and more solicitous. You two had met at a convention the year before and immediately taken a liking to each other. You see how I remember everything you tell me! I even remember you said he looked like you with his mustache and hair still dark (one way or another). Already, he'd gotten you a ticket to one of the Cirque de Soleil shows playing at the Strip for the night after your reading. At the airport, filled with slot machines and showgirls, he gave you a warm hug."

You could see and even feel that hug from Bennet again but with it the image of David suddenly faded to extinction and the horror movie came rushing back. You let the letter flutter to the floor then like a giant, indoor snowflake—a Las Vegas snowflake. Then you kicked it like a bug. You felt betrayed because you'd hoped the letter would give you an escape by making you think of your brother. Instead, it only re-stimulated and intensified your Vegas memories. Moreover, you were too tired and overwhelmed to struggle against that now and had already surrendered to the idea of going over everything in the movie one more time in the hopes of finally exhausting it. You were also still seeing and feeling the hug—whether you closed your eyes or not—and hearing Bennet say once more during your drive into town, "I'm sorry we couldn't get you a better hotel, but at least it's within walking distance of the Strip."

You remember that you actually thought the hotel charming. With its low to the ground design, earth-tone colors, palm trees and outdoor swimming pool it reminded you of a California hotel. Your brother was right in a way—all things considered, you were in pretty good spirits when you arrived. David was a lawyer and was careful and often accurate, though in a limited sense, with his observations. For instance, from an "objective" point of view your reading was a success. There was a good-sized crowd (considering your books aren't commercial and you were reading from a short-story collection), "spontaneously warm applause" and then the added glamorous touch of those cable T.V. cameras focusing on you. All of this was heady stuff for you who were used to 20 or 30 people at most of your readings and naturally this gratified you. You even remembered wishing David were at this reading, as he had often been before in lieu of your professionally preoccupied parents. But it was also equally true, and this David would never understand, that on another level the "warm applause" tortured you, that what you wanted instead was a shocked explosion from the audience because you wanted to change their lives, not just make them appreciate another "good" writer. Though you never felt this when you went to other writers' readings, that was no consolation at all. Because you didn't transform your audience in any way, you felt a kind of depression gnawing at you. Given your age and your cancer you probably never would, so you looked to women, once again, to give you an injection of the kind of excitement your work had once more failed to provide. You didn't have to wait too long.

After the reading, Bennet took you to dinner at a Thai restaurant with a group of university professor/writers and a couple of graduate students. One of the students was a part Thai, part American named Maya. She was quite pretty and energetic with a secretive side that appealed to you. You were attracted to her, but she was young enough to be your daughter so you were careful not to let yourself get too encouraged. But soon she mentioned a quasi-famous poet/ professor old enough to be your father, who had once taught both of you, albeit at different times and at different universities, and she said twice that the whole term she'd had a mad crush on him. From that moment on (as the song goes) you virtually ignored the other people at the table and focused on her.

Because of the fear you had after learning your biopsy results and the torturous decision you had to make about what kind of treatment to pursue for your prostate cancer, you were on a new medication for anxiety that gave you a kind of instant social courage. You also had two or three drinks. She was drinking, too, though less ardently than you, but seemed eager enough to answer all your questions. She said she was lonely and felt completely disconnected from Las Vegas. She didn't even know how to drive. She'd been living near Boston before, where driving a car wasn't that important. She went to the university at Las Vegas a year and a half ago because she'd won a fellowship there that was now essentially what she was living off.

"That's why I didn't buy your book," she said, a little ruefully.

You told her that, of course, you would give her a copy of your book. You said, don't you have lots of friends, perhaps you also said "admirers" in an obvious allusion to how attractive she was (though she was definitely more attractive in a New England than a Vegas kind of way). She said she stayed home almost every night and had never even seen much of the Strip. She'd had a hard enough time adjusting to Boston once she came to the States but the Vegas sensibility was still alien to her. Interesting to observe, she said, but impossible to feel at home in.

"But what will you do? You have to get out of here." (Come with me, you wanted to say because, though you are over 50, your romantic fantasies are as frequent and extreme as a 16 year olds'.)

What you did say was that you wanted to see the Bellagio and the other great hotels and why didn't she go with you after dinner so you could see them together and, who knows, maybe even gamble a little.

"As long as you're living in a place you may as well see what it's famous for," you said.

"Sure, why not?" she said, smiling. She seemed charmed by you, maybe also impressed by your writing, maybe not, but definitely charmed, which was more important to you these days when your sexual future was so uncertain because of your cancer and the present seemed to be all one had.

"Just don't let me lose too much of my money," she said.

"We'll only gamble with mine," you assured her.

At this point, you remembered that the aging poet to your left interrupted you and started asking you some questions. It was all you could do not to snap at him. You assumed, at first, that he was making nice because he wanted you to arrange a similar type of reading for him at your university—something you figured you only owed Bennet, your host. But a few minutes later he began directing his conversation at Maya. It was soon obvious that he was trying to hit on her as well despite the fact that his dowdy wife was seated immediately to his left. Those were difficult moments—as was the whole rest of the dinner, followed by the obligatory, absurdly prolonged goodbyes in the parking lot. But, you reminded yourself, it was really like one of those televised storm warnings where the storm never materializes, and when you and Maya rode in Bennet's car while he drove you up the Strip amidst much good cheer and joking and deposited you at one of the entrances of the Bellagio, you were feeling giddy again.

The big hotels of Las Vegas are not so much hotels as worlds (each with its own theme) which they were not shy about announcing either with giant fountains and sculptures of faux rockets or with golden pharaohs and sphinxes. In one world, you saw a giant replica of the most famous landmarks of New York that went on for a block, including a "Coney Island" amusement park replete with roaring rollercoaster and screaming children.

The Bellagio was supposed to be the classiest of the hotels but, like so much of Vegas, its beauty was inseparable from its vulgarity. In its casino, as in all Las Vegas casinos, you entered an underground world without time, where clocks were as absent as the sky, just in case knowledge or even dim awareness of time might distract the gamblers from the steady stream of money they were pumping into the slots or black jack tables.

The two of you walked around this maze, alternately appalled and delighted. You walked almost a mile before settling at a little bar at a far end of the casino. It was clear by now that neither of you had an interest in gambling, but you wanted to drink and even more to have her drink.

"Well," you said, indicating the giant space around you, "bright lights, big city."

She laughed and, naturally, you liked that.

You finally persuaded her to drink a Manhattan. You joined her with another vodka tonic. Since there was so little alcohol in the drinks you knew it would take a while to loosen her up. You began to ask her questions, specifically about her childhood, then, later, after her second drink, about her past love life. Like most lonely people she was eager to talk and was soon describing life in a rural Thai village. You told yourself to listen closely, to really try to understand this person, but it was difficult, like listening to someone explain how to do a puzzle without being able to quite understand where to put a few key pieces. It was not that her story was boring or without revelations. You could sense, for example, when she described her intensely ambivalent relationship with her American father who'd died of a heart attack a few years ago why she gravitated towards older men. You tried harder to concentrate as she described her few lovers, including the main one with whom she'd broken up and reconciled a number of times and who still called her. He was a foreigner—part Oriental, part Hispanic. She told you more than once where he was from, as well as his name, but you couldn't remember either no matter how angry it made you not to know. You thought of how Maya lived in a separate continent from you because of her background and age. Then you started thinking about the invisible life of your cells and the way they'd turned against you in your prostate and tried to remember something David had written you about courage. That made you take another drink. You put your hand on her shoulder, briefly touched her hair. She didn't respond although she didn't say or do anything to stop you.

Finally, you paid for the drinks and said, "Let's take a walk." The bartender was starting to talk too much to Maya—as if he were the son of the professor/poet in the restaurant—and you were relieved when she said she wanted to walk too.

Meanwhile you popped another pill and a few minutes later finally felt the high you'd been hoping for. Almost immediately you realized you were lost, but you didn't care.

"It's like Halloween in here."

"That's what Vegas is," she said, "Halloween 24/7."

The next thing you knew you were walking

through an elaborately rendered faux Parisian village replete with its bistros and patisseries. It vaguely occurred to you that you might now be in a different hotel, but it hardly mattered.

Then you began to offer some unsolicited insights about her ex-boyfriend's on-again, off-again behavior. You felt that as the older, presumably wiser person you were expected to use your presumptive power of mature advice as a way to demonstrate how she could benefit by hanging out with you. Maya listened to you closely as you enunciated, as well as the vodkas and Xanax in your body would permit, your relationship advice.

The truth is your own advice soon bored you and during the last half of your speech you were already thinking again about the different cancer treatments available to you; radioactive seed versus radical prostatectomy versus laparoscopic surgery. David naturally advised you to take the most conservative approach which was open surgery and you had in fact ultimately listened to him and made an appointment with a surgeon. But you continued to think about alternative treatments anyway. Remembering all this you realized that talking alone wasn't going to help you get through this night. Moreover, with your girlfriend Margo essentially estranged from you this was possibly your last real chance to make love in your life.

"Oh, this is lovely," you said about an outdoor "French café" you two just discovered under a cleverly constructed "chestnut tree."

"Let's have one more drink."

"I think I'm pretty high," Maya said.

"Nowhere near enough."

"I don't know."

"You're being far too rational, especially for a poet."

"But I write fiction," she said, correcting you as she sat down at the table.

You felt a tinge of pain or something like it. You hated it when people caught you not listening to them, especially since you couldn't stand it when they didn't listen to you.

"But all fiction writers want to be thought of as poets or at least as being poetic," you said, trying to recover. "Wasn't it Faulkner who said 'every novelist is a failed poet'?"

She laughed. "That's a good saying. Did you used to write poetry, too?"

"Oh sure. Wrote it, failed at it, abysmally, then gave it up permanently for fiction at which I also failed, though less spectacularly."

She laughed. She was on your side again and soon agreed to have a drink. You realized now that you not only were attracted to her but liked her too, and you reached across the table and touched her hair. She let you, at least for a few seconds, then the waitress appeared, with half her tits showing, took your order for drinks, and everything seemed right for a moment.

But nothing ever stayed the same in Vegas for very long, as if each roll of the dice revealed how time changed every moment. It was like cancer that way, too, although cancer changed much more slowly, at least in the beginning.

You waited till you were both through with your next drink—sensing that at last she was high—before you touched her hair again and part of her face. She didn't respond as you hoped, but she let you do it. You pictured your hotel room with its pathetic television and you knew you needed her there with you—could already picture what you'd do in bed together.

"I really like you," you said. "Do you think you like me?"

She hesitated—and you decided not to let her answer.

"As soon as we started talking in the restaurant I sensed a connection between us, didn't you?" you said, appalled by how trite you sounded.

She half nodded and finished her drink.

"It's so rare that that happens, so I think you have to act upon it when it does. It's just crazy and tragic really when people don't. I mean we're all gonna die in such a short time—yet people hold back out of fear and pride—that's the insanity of it."

You were aware that you were rambling and still sounded like an old hippie but in a way you thought that might help win her over—to show her that inside, once she got past your aging face and body, you were young and in certain ways even younger than her.

"Don't you feel that way about me too? Tell me the truth."

"I feel a connection…"

"Good, me too," you said, touching her just above her knee.

"Can I ask you something?" she said.

"Sure."

"How old are you?"

It was, of course, the worst question she could have asked. You wanted to yell at her, There's no time here so why are you asking me that?

"Oh God, let's see, I think I'm 2006," you said, making her laugh. "Hey, it's getting really hot in here, have you noticed? Let's take a walk, okay? Let's take a walk together."

So after you both finished your drinks and you paid up, you two started walking again through the remains of the French village. But walking wasn't really what you wanted to do, and soon you began putting your hands on her and telling her how much you liked her again.

"I think that's your drink talking," she said, slipping away from you. "I think you're just very high."

"No," you protested. "Just very attracted to you."

She was walking ahead of you, and you struggled to catch up.

"I have to get home now," she said, avoiding your eyes. "It's getting late."

You saw then that it was hopeless and told her you'd get her a cab. Then you asked a couple of people how to get out of the hotel and set about trying to follow their directions.

It's amazing how quickly people disappear—first from your sight, then from your mind (which takes a little longer) and then from the earth itself.

You were outside the Bellagio waiting for a cab. The strange beauty of the Strip flared up at you—the lights and trees and fountains.

You both commented on it before you got in the taxi.

You wouldn't touch her again; you wouldn't put either of you through that. Instead you sat a polite distance apart and asked a few more questions about her school and thought about your cancer, and when it was time for her to get out, you actually shook hands with her before getting back in the cab and telling the driver to take you to your hotel, which was a relatively short distance away.

But once you were back inside your room you immediately began to panic. It was so small and forlorn like your own personal section of hell, and it only had those three idiotic channels.

With nothing to distract you, you began thinking about your different prostate options. If you chose brachytherapy and had the radioactive seeds implanted you might have minimal side effects, and if you were one of the lucky ones, which the brachytherapists placed at 70%, you might never miss a beat in your sex life, and even if you were one of the unlucky 30% there'd usually be a grace period of a year or so before you'd become impotent. The brachytherapists had just published a study saying their twelve-year survival rates were comparable to open surgery but the surgeons weren't buying it, at least not publicly. While conceding that the five-year rates were comparable, they said the long term data wasn't sufficient to compare it to the "gold standard" of radical retropubic prostatectomy. What "gold standard" you asked yourself, as you paced around your room—the gold standard of castration?

It was too excruciating to think about. You took yet another Xanax, then not much later another, turned on the TV, lay down and thought about Maya. When that soon proved too painful you thought about David instead. That was easier, especially when you concentrated on your relatively happy childhood, and you soon closed your eyes.

You could remember again the kingdom that you shared with him. You were two little kings in a white palace with a yard lined by trees and flowers which magically expanded, it seemed, to accommodate your endless games of baseball and badminton, hide and seek, and snowballs and sledding downhill on your Christmas sleds or sometimes just on garbage can covers—the wind in your face the whole way.

Inside the house you two played your

games of chance: Parcheesi and Monopoly, Gin Rummy and Fish or just rolling dice—the eternal game, it turns out, in Las Vegas (just as in your life, which would be nothing now but a game of chance forever). Cards were fascinating then, as were raisins, hearts of celery and lettuce, the roots of carrots, long banisters and enormous chairs and closets that stored toys and hid witches. As your older brother by two years, David protected you from the witches as he continued to try to do throughout your life.

You thought a little more about him but you had a restless spirit and body—it's what often made you identify with ghosts. This time you suddenly rose from your bed of death, as you thought of it, and the next thing you knew you were on the streets heading towards Maya's apartment, moving as fast as you'd ever moved in your life. "I have cancer but I'm flying," you thought. Nothing, not your humiliation, your age, your brother, or your cancer would stop you now. Then you thought of the lines from Dylan Thomas: "Because their words had forked no lightening / they do not go gentle into that good night." If your words at the reading had forked lightning, Maya wouldn't have resisted you, instead you would have forked her. But now your action would fork lightning because nothing would stop you.

You wondered briefly if you could get inside her building—yet in a moment that problem disappeared when an elderly man leaving the building at the same moment you were trying to enter held the door open to let you in. You thanked him and went directly to her apartment where you knocked but got no answer, then found yourself listening at the door for signs of her. "It's Darren," you finally said. "Can I talk to you?"

You anticipated more resistance but she opened the door, wearing a bathrobe.

"What are you doing?" she said.

But you didn't feel you had to answer that question as you began to unfasten her robe, and felt her slender, squirming body beneath it. "So this is what rape is," you thought just before the door opened again and a man entered the room. Was it her longtime Hispanic/Oriental lover; was it, inexplicably, David?

...You opened your eyes, the TV was on and you were still in your hotel bed but no one was with you. It took you quite a while to understand your dream and even that what had happened was in a dream contained, as it was, like a subset within the larger dream of your life, yet different from it. Perhaps it was caused by overmedicating yourself, perhaps you were even half awake and guiding the events as you never can do in a real dream. All you knew was it was 3:45 a.m., and you were wide awake with nothing watchable on TV and no possibility of sleeping. There was no one you could phone, either, because you were in a different time zone from anyone you knew. Of course, you could have called your brother but you didn't think of him as someone you could benefit from calling. It's the weirdest thing. At first, you never think you can confide in him, but later when your troubles thicken and some permanent damage has already been done, you end up telling him everything. But this didn't occur to you then. He wasn't even a blip on your radar screen. There was nothing on your radar screen (not even Maya despite your recent "dream"). Nothing but the desire to get high so you could fall back asleep. You weren't even scheduled for any human contact until three o'clock tomorrow afternoon when you and Bennet were supposed to drive to the mountains.

(You would end up cancelling that event as well as the Cirque du Soleil with the excuse of "mild food poisoning").

Originally, Maya was going to go with you and Bennet to the mountains, but there was little chance of that now. Sizing everything up, you put your clothes on, including your new brown leather jacket because it made you feel tough and confident, rinsed your mouth, swallowed a Viagra and hit the streets.

When you were first dropped off at your hotel and had a few hours to kill before your reading, you'd walked around your neighborhood and noticed three things: all the free sex flyers in the newspaper stands with photos of various girls who would "dance" for you in your room (you collected quite a number of those), a couple of hookers walking the street who looked like crack whores, and a twenty-four hour convenience store where they sold alcohol. You cursed yourself for not thinking ahead and buying something to drink earlier—although the refrigerator in your room wasn't working so whatever you drank would be warm.

You bought a couple of large cans of beer and started walking back to your room when you saw a hooker. She was black and a little chunky and the two of you walked up to each other simultaneously. She said her name was Pandora. Her blouse was low cut and her belly button was sticking out, but otherwise there was nothing whorish about her. She was overweight and not much more than average looking, though of course she was young enough to be your daughter and therefore attractive for that reason alone.

"I got a room at a hotel a couple blocks from here," you said.

When she asked you what you wanted to

do you said you just wanted to spend some time with her.

"I cost a hundred an hour."

"Okay. You got some weed? I need to get high to get back to sleep."

"I got something."

"Great," you said. "My name is Darren."

"That's a nice jacket," she said, rubbing her fingers up and down one of your arms. You were doubly glad now that you wore it.

"Follow a little behind me till we get to my hotel, okay?"

"No problem."

While you were walking you wondered if you were doing anything wrong about Margo—your probably ex-girlfriend—and decided that given all the fights and things you'd said to each other, especially since your cancer, the relationship was definitely broken forever just like your penis would soon be broken no matter what treatment you chose. David, of course, had lived very differently than you—getting married and spending so many years with the same woman—but he'd wound up divorced, alone, and childless like you so what was the difference? At any rate, you thought of a form of sex not involving intercourse where Pandora wouldn't even have to touch your penis. You thought of it in a general way and by the time you got to your room through a side entrance to the hotel—a gate that your key could open—you had essentially finalized the details.

"You wanna pay me a hundred up front?"

You thought you would get right to the sex idea you had that would protect you and conceivably Margo, in the unlikely event you ever saw her again, but Pandora noticed the book you'd read from at the university on the floor. Your picture, from a number of years ago, was on the back cover.

"You write this book?" she said.

"I plead guilty."

"That your picture there?"

"From a younger, happier time. This way my readers will think I'm younger. You see, in my books I never age."

"That's smart. You make some money from it?"

"Not very much. It's gotten some good reviews though," you couldn't resist mentioning.

"Read me something from the book," she'd said. "I don't read too good."

You read a few pages and just as you were beginning to get into it you could see that she was losing interest.

"So, you get the general idea," you said, closing the book.

She nodded sullenly. She didn't seem impressed.

"So you got some pot or ...."

"Right here mister," she said, handing you a crudely made pipe with tin foil or something like it around the opening.

"What is this? Is this crack?" you said, as you inhaled. You'd never smoked crack, at least not knowingly, but you were desperate to get high.

She shrugged sullenly again as if it were too much trouble to answer your question.

"You ain't smoking it right, mister. You not inhaling it right. You're wasting it," she said angrily, as if you'd committed a crime. "Here," she said, taking the pipe from you, "like this."

You tried to imitate her, but she still seemed to disapprove. Nevertheless you felt something good, though it went away after a minute.

You told her about your sex idea and she agreed to it and told you the price. She did it for a little while—but you weren't able to come, not even close. You were thinking about the crack that filled you with such a rich feeling for a minute.

"Let's smoke some more," you said.

According to her, you did it wrong again but you felt a blissful high for a few minutes during which you not only became affectionate but started talking to her in your seriously earnest, old hippie way about "throwing away our masks" and "getting to the essence" of each other. But just as you felt your two souls merging your high began to wear off.

"Let's smoke some more," you said.

"We all out mister. I don't got no more."

"Shit," you said. You stood up and paced.

She gave you a funny look then said, "I can get some more. I'll call someone on my cell, the girl I live with, and she'll bring it to the store where I met you."

"Why can't she bring it here?"

"She won't go to no hotel, that's my job. Just give me some money, and I'll bring it back to you," Pandora said.

"No, no," you said, still pacing. "I'll go with you. When I see her I'll give you the money."

"Don't you trust me?"

"I just want to do it this way," you said, convinced you were making the only reasonable decision.

She made her phone call, and the two of you got dressed. You kept feeling for the fifties in your pocket to be sure they were still there.

When you got outside she said, "I'm cold. Let me wear your jacket."

You took it off and gave it to her. She was a woman, after all, and you'd always been polite to women and always tried to please them your whole life long, even more than you tried to get them to please you. If David saw you do it, he would approve.

You were walking through the outdoor gardens of the hotel. The leaves blown by the wind made you think of radioactive seeds. You thought you were walking fast, but she was walking ahead of you, and you had to constantly increase your speed to keep up with her.

You felt a little cold without your jacket but were glad you'd given it to her—especially considering how skimpily she was dressed.

When you reached the convenience store you pulled up next to her.

"When will she be here?" you said.

"She in the store already. You stay outside. You'll make her nervous."

"Why? Why can't I go in the store?"

"I told you, that ain't the deal. Don't worry, I'll be back in a minute."

You let her go then or, more probably, she simply walked ahead of you into the store and you paced around and waited on the sidewalk in front of the door. Time slowed down then like music suddenly getting slower or maybe it was just that you started thinking about your cancer again. A moment later you walked into the store and saw Pandora talking with a fatter, Hispanic looking woman in a big white sweater.

As soon as Pandora saw you, she started walking towards the door, her friend walking just ahead of her. Pandora gave you a dirty look, while the friend ignored you.

"Did you get it?" you said, but Pandora said nothing until you got out on the street. "You wait here, it's in her car."

You stood still, confused for a second. On the one hand it made sense that her roommate didn't want to deal with you—a stranger—in anything to do with drugs, so for a while you did as you were told and waited. Then you thought about your three hundred dollar jacket that Pandora was still wearing and you started walking after them, then running. You saw them get into a white station wagon, caught a glimpse of the Hispanic woman who looked at you through the window with a kind of serenely sad expression before they sped away up the street.

You were alone again, without your jacket. You were too dazed to be angry but soon you were angry. You remember thinking that you couldn't end the night that way, getting ripped-off like that, losing the jacket that you'd bought to wear in Vegas because, in spite of your cancer, it made you feel important in some vague way.

A few minutes went by. You realized you were walking to your hotel as if the whores might still meet you there, then walking back to the store as if they might come back to you in the station wagon. It took that long before you realized you really had been robbed.

Then you remembered the other crack whore you saw during your walk (before your reading) in the afternoon. Thin and almost demented looking like a zombie—yet she'd smiled at you, and you were surprised to discover that she had all her teeth.

You found yourself going back to the spot where you remembered seeing her because you knew prostitutes were very territorial so you circled around her spot a couple of times, and in a few minutes you saw her again in front of the convenience store with her big bug out eyes, birdlike nose and ghost-thin body. She said her name was Robin, but she looked more like a sandpiper. She was the homeliest prostitute you'd ever seen yet you were attracted to her in a way simply because she was another resident from the distant continent of youth, young enough to be your daughter, once more and therefore innocent in a way and sympathetic when she talked. You soon found yourself telling her you'd just been robbed.

"You're not gonna do that to me, are you?" you said.

"No, no, I'm a good person," Robin said.

The negotiations went quickly. As far as you knew, you were sticking to your safe sex plan.

When you were inside the room she saw your book and acted impressed but it now had a bitter memory connected to it because of Pandora, so you quickly changed the subject.

You'd already told her what you wanted her to do and for a hundred dollars she'd agreed to do it. Then, for a while she did do it, but it didn't work. You were on the bed, still a little high, realizing that what you'd instructed her to do wasn't going to give you enough stimulation to come, and that what you really needed to bury this night of escalating failures was to smoke some more till you'd be able to come or at least pass out.

"You got some pot or something else we can smoke?" you said, turning to face her in bed.

"I'll make it up," she said, referring to her pipe which she suddenly produced like a magician. This in itself didn't surprise you since no one was able to hide more things or make them suddenly appear than hookers—they were all like magicians that way.

You were glad it was crack. You'd never had it before Pandora and the memory of the feeling was still there. You and Robin sat on the bed sharing her hastily improvised crack pipe. She was more patient than Pandora, but you were still inept— probably because you were too eager to inhale and also because you had to inhale it differently than marijuana and weren't used to it.

"Wait," she said. "Let me get it first, then you inhale it from my mouth."

This immediately struck you as dangerous—open mouth contact like that—but you couldn't resist getting high from the crack and so your mouths did the transfer three or four times, and you did get high. It felt like your first success of the night. It seemed unbelievable to you as you quickly thought of your long history with women and all the times you'd gotten high with them that you'd never taken a really dangerous drug like crack before. And the way you'd done it, taking it from her mouth like an infant being fed by his mother was somehow erotic and touching at the same time.

The next thing you knew you were giving her head, licking her all over her pussy (though you checked her out first and saw no signs of blood or lesions or anything else suspicious looking) until she finally came in your mouth. It was odd how your brain was split in two about this. Part of you felt it was something you shouldn't be doing but the wish to please her and do it was stronger. It was your vanity you supposed or your lifelong training in always trying to please women and, through them, yourself.

"That felt so good. I haven't had that in so long," Robin said, right after her orgasm.

You were glad but you wanted yours, too. So far you'd spent or lost about three hundred dollars, plus lost your leather jacket—the best piece of clothing you owned and had almost nothing to show for it.

"I want you to suck me now too," you said, leading her by the hand to the bathroom.

"Sure," she said. "I'm gonna do it real good till you go crazy."

You positioned her on the toilet seat, stood over her and in just the right amount of time came fully and strongly in her mouth, until you did scream out loud—the first natural sound you'd made in Las Vegas—maybe the first natural sound you'd made since you found out you had cancer.

It was while you were both dressing in the half light of your room that you noticed again how skinny she was and asked her if she had HIV.

"No, I don't have it."

"How do you know?

"I get checked at a clinic every three weeks," she said, making eye contact with you. It was the standard hooker answer (one you'd heard before), but it was said so smoothly that it made you distrust her, especially since your high was wearing off, and you were beginning to get nervous.

You dressed quietly for awhile. If you were in a park you could probably hear the wind moving through the leaves. Instead you heard a strange little music coming from the air conditioner. You missed your high already—what was the point of such feelings if they lasted such a short time and then returned you so abruptly to the regular world of worry?

She, however, was acting quite cheerful. Did that mean she was still on her high, you wondered jealously? You began thinking dark thoughts again, the kind David would ridicule, and started asking her questions to try to distract yourself from them.

Robin was quite willing to talk. She told you she had a regular job, well maybe more like a part-time job working behind a counter. She said she only hooked about once a month and that she had a 16-year-old daughter who was a good artist.

"Don't you think it's kind of dangerous to go out on the streets like that? I mean, not everyone is as nice as me," you said.

"Hey, you know what, I got bigger things to worry about, so now I just let myself relax when I work."

"What are those bigger things?"

"For one thing, I got brain cancer. Here," she said, walking ghostlike towards you, "feel this lump." She took your hand and placed it on the lump. You felt it and clearly saw it on her head. It was substantial and a look of fear must have covered your face.

"Don't worry, you won't get it. You're smart enough to know it's not contagious, aren't you? They told me it's inoperable, so now I don't worry anymore like I used to, and I just have fun. Why are you looking at me that way?"

"Cause people get cancer from having AIDS, and I have cancer too, prostate cancer, and now I'm worried that I might have gotten AIDS, too."

She sat down on the bed again and attended to her shoes and stockings.

"Well, I don't have HIV," she said, but more softly this time, with her eyes cast down at the floor.

I've killed myself twice, you thought. Once slowly over time because I was unlucky and the second time with one bad decision in a single night. It was all you could think about and when she asked you if you wanted her to get more crack so you two could do it again you could barely concentrate enough to shake your head and say no.

You did manage to be polite and pay her another hundred—she'd kept to her word after all, and it was theoretically possible that she'd told you the truth. She offered you her phone number but instead you gave her yours. You remember thinking that you could ask her a thousand times if she had AIDS or HIV, and her answer would be the same, and you would never believe it anyway. You had already been robbed by one prostitute; it only made sense that you'd be lied to by another.

Then Robin left your room but, like a true ghost, didn't completely vanish. Immediately you began reviewing everything you two did, checking it for exposure to HIV, as if going over and over a videotape. It was then you began to panic and called your brother and told him what happened in one mad rush of speech.

When you got off the phone with David you were perspiring heavily through your shirt. You had called him out of reflex perhaps, but you'd still hoped for some relief. Yet you didn't feel better and immediately regretted that you'd told him so much. What if he did come looking for you? The thought of David in Las Vegas was... essentially unthinkable...but so was having your surgery in Philadelphia, so was being tested for HIV. That's when you visited Sid at the registration desk and paid him the money to tell your brother you weren't in, came back to the room and began watching the 48-hour horror movie, only leaving to eat at the nearest fast food places you could find in the opposite direction from where the hookers were.

...Now, still in your room, with David's letter on the floor, you were once more seeing images of Robin's and Pandora's faces flickering on and off in front of you like giant fireflies. This made you pace faster as if you thought that by increasing the speed of your steps you could somehow outrun them. But you couldn't outrun them or the thoughts attached to them that seemed fastened to their firefly wings. You tried to conjure up your "girlfriend" Margo, but you couldn't do that either, and when you could retrieve a kind of blurry image for a few moments, it made you feel worse.

You took a drink of warm beer and another pill. You couldn't decide—drink or pill, pill or drink—so you did both. Then by sheer force of will you were able to "see" Maya's face and for some reason immediately you felt some relief.

Of course you had probably ruined things with her by coming on to her so soon but maybe not. She'd already been through a number of things for a woman her age, and maybe she could forgive you. In fact, it suddenly seemed possible that she already had and was perhaps regretting running away from you so soon. Maybe that's why you "dreamed" of her in the way you did. But how could you know? You couldn't unless you spoke to her or better still, saw her. But did you even remember where she lived—you were not after all the world's greatest when it came to directions;, that was David's department. You closed your eyes unusually tight to concentrate on where the cab had dropped her off and eventually decided that you would know how to get there. Besides, during your walkabout through the hotels, you'd gotten her address. But where exactly had you put it?

For the next few minutes you made a frenzied search through your room only to discover that the address was in the back pocket of your pants (you'd even remembered the apartment 2B part correctly in your "dream"). What else was in your pocket you wondered as you once more rinsed your mouth with hydrogen peroxide, put on the one sports jacket you had brought and went out on the street. Would you ever get off it, you thought, the street that had already killed you a second time tonight? But it wasn't just Las Vegas, you realized. When you lived in Philadelphia and before that in New York, you often walked the streets at night looking for whatever it was you were looking for, sometimes hookers, sometimes a drink or just someone to talk to. What you did in Las Vegas wasn't really so different, was, in fact, a well-practiced part of your life.

"You die of your life," you said to yourself as you got in a cab and gave the driver Maya's address. And then you laughed out loud a little at your pomposity and aphorism addiction and at David's remark that "you should have been born in ancient Greece." In fact, because of your laughter you had to repeat your somewhat impressionistic directions to the driver.

Probably from listening to people like you before, people a little confused and panicky who were losing whatever game of chance they were playing, your driver asked you if you wanted him to wait for you. You should have said yes, but pride and sheer impulse made you say it wasn't necessary. Instead, you stepped out of the cab onto a dark street, far away from the Strip, and began moving gingerly toward Maya's apartment building. It was strange, as you got closer the "distance" between you two got even further. You realized there were no words you could say that could explain what you felt. She was truly in a different continent from you, and yours was the Continent of Cancer—which was sometimes a Tropic of Cancer, sometimes a South Pole of Cancer through which a glacier of HIV was now slowly beginning to float, as well.

You thought of calling her but knew that wouldn't make a difference either so you walked past her building heading towards what you hoped would be a main street or at least a bigger street of some kind where you could get a cab. If not you might have to walk back to your hotel somehow or try to find a new hotel if you got lost. The temperature had dropped rapidly, and you began to shiver. After another block, you put your hands deep inside your jacket pockets to warm them up. In your right pocket you felt something you immediately withdrew, though you had to walk to a rare street lamp before you could see it. It was the long letter from David, which unwittingly you'd taken with you.

This time you read the whole letter from beginning to end, wondering why you'd avoided doing that for nearly two days and had instead read it before in a fragmentary, almost cubistic way. The letter was overwrought and sentimental, earnest and didactic—it was many things you decided. Reading it carefully you found the line about courage you'd tried to remember earlier. "Courage, in the end, is all we have, Darren, it's even more important than our identity."

What did this mean? Did it mean anything? Was the lawyer simply trying to be poetic? Did he really just want to help you? You didn't know, but reading it (and the whole letter) seemed to make your hands warmer. You had shivered and now you'd stopped shivering. You were alone in the dark, but you didn't feel too alone—and that was because of your brother. Then you walked back as quickly as you could to the hotel.

At the registration desk, Sid looked up from his racing form when you walked into the deserted lobby. "This place is evil," you muttered almost loud enough for him to hear. Because you'd once paid him off to misinform your brother, you now had enough value for him to look up and talk to you.

"Can I help you, my friend?" he said.

You stared at him thinking of all the hookers, all the death in short skirts he'd let walk by him into the hotel, and you tried to burn your eyes into his being.

"I'm checking out, going home," you said, surprised that you even bothered to explain anything to him. But, of course, he was a man and required some kind of explanation.

"Very good, sir," he said, forcing a smile.

"Yes, it's all very good," you added, unable to resist the irony because you are a writer and always thought of yourself as an irony connoisseur.

FROM THE DIARY OF AN INVALID

The healthy body is the great diverter from thinking about the world. The invalid, however, has little to do besides think, often about finding ways to move around his home, which has now become a kind of obstacle course.

I'm trying not to be a bore in my journal, at least, like other people with limited mobility who endlessly describe their symptoms and lack of progress. I'm trying not to bore myself. Nevertheless, I need to make a few observations. When you can't run any longer or even walk for any distance at a normal speed, you have memories of running or of taking long, leisurely walks—memories that occur without warning. And when you don't have memories, you begin dreaming more than you ever have but never about your actual condition.

. . . I'm lying on my back on a special couch that's been adapted for the purpose of watching my young son, Andy, running back and forth from the family room where I am (and where I

spend 80% of my time watching TV or sleeping)
through what used to be my office to the living
room and back. He runs with a kind of frenzied
ecstasy, arms raised and waving like a receiver
trying to show his quarterback that he's open.
When I'm not remembering, I watch him running.
It always puts a smile on my face. Later we tell
stories together about an imaginary world we've
co-created. Our stories about this world have
been going on for years.

. . . About nine months ago I began to feel a
sharp, sciatica-type pain in both my thighs. The
pain was intermittent but severe enough that I
finally went to an orthopedist. The x-rays he took
revealed a degenerative disk in my back. The
doctor then explained the concept of "referred
pain" to me (i.e. the problem actually originated
in my lower back but I "felt" the pain in my legs).
He said that could explain the leg pain "from an
orthopedic point of view." However, he strongly
suggested that I see a neurologist. I ended up
seeing three of them as well as two internists
and two "Pain Management Specialists." It all
quickly became a maze of contradictions and
confusion like trying to make sense of a world
deeply underwater. One said I was suffering
from "pre-diabetic neuropathy." One diagnosed
me with Parkinson's, another said he thought
I had Restless Leg Syndrome. Others said they
simply didn't know what I was suffering from.
The invalid has to learn to live with mystery,
including the mystery of doctors and how little
they listen, how little they know. Meanwhile,
my pain, and especially my weakness, was
increasing steadily. Finally, I started a series of
epidurals, which so far have brought me some
relief from pain and a small increase in strength.

Also, I managed to get a medical leave of absence from work through I continue to co-parent Andy (who is with me half the time—I wish it were all the time) with his mother, who lives less than two miles away.

When Andy is at school or at his mother's I retreat more into my past. Many of my memories are of times when I could run and jump or otherwise move freely. I have lots of memories of basketball that I played mostly on outdoor playgrounds in Philadelphia and New York and at other times in my life in Santa Monica or in St. Louis where I live now. They are short memories because I try to shut them down but part of my brain must need to remember them, must cling to them like a desperate lover.

TV is a fairly reliable memory killer, as it's a thought killer in general, but I can't watch it, or movies, all the time. I sometimes try lying on my bed and listening to music on my CD player. Often it makes me think of women in my past, particularly of places I went to with them on vacations, and I'll be flooded with longing or regret. I've learned to avoid the very composers I love the most like Mahler and Prokofiev because they're now too painful to listen to. Other times, I lie in bed and read a little, until that gets too uncomfortable, or else lie in silence and then I often begin to remember my mother and sister and lately many memories of my father. At times, these memories fuse with my dreams and when they're over it's hard to tell which it was. Did I really once run around the house with him? Did we really once routinely play Chinese checkers or chess? (I have many memories of serious conversations with my father but very few of playing with him.) Did I also occasionally sneak into his closet and steal the change from his sports jacket? And could I really have snuck into his bed when I couldn't sleep? Something he later told me I could always do.

My father was a successful man but a modest one. He was born in Poland, near Warsaw, and didn't come to the United States until he was 21. Yet he spoke perfect (though heavily accented) English. He was a gentle man and a short man, but he was strong and had an iron will. He was the eldest of four brothers and a sister but outlived them all (two brothers were killed by the Nazis). He never went to high school, but he could speak seven languages. He knew a lot about politics, music, philosophy, and had, himself, quite a philosophical kind of mind. "Art is the last illusion" he told me, eternal life being the first. He also once said "fame and Christmas are for children."

My father had me late in life, and I was always worried about him dying, though he lived till I was 33. I also am an older father and wonder lately if Andy has similar anxieties about me. My father would have loved Andy, I'm sure, but he never lived to see him. My mother did but by the time Andy was two or three she was already suffering from dementia, dictating repetitive incomprehensible messages from her chair, which she sometimes thought was a car, just as she sometimes thought I was her husband.

When you are an invalid you live profoundly separated from the rest of able-bodied people regardless of how often you spend time with them. Very shortly after your illness strikes, you realize that no matter how genuinely sympathetic or curious people are, they can never understand what you're feeling (which you yourself can't describe), either physically or emotionally. Unless it's happened to them recently, the only thing other people can really understand is a cold.

In the case of Andy, he's said nothing about it and I prefer it that way. It would interfere with our stories and joking. Lately, an important shift in our ongoing story has occurred! Some of our main characters, including Garret J. Gunderhold, have left Rinaldia and/or Rhodnesia (both countries in the continent of Crasia) for the United States. It's the first time in years that our story is taking place in a real country. Moreover Gunderhold, an international criminal, movie producer, and amusement park mogul has returned to his original position (when he was known as Aaron Wadimer and lived in the Crasian country of Wadova) as headmaster of a boarding school. Gunderhold, a ruthlessly ambitious sociopath, who loves fame and power and will do anything to get it, now wants to run the most prestigious and profitable private school in the U.S. and has established in Vermont The Gunderhold Academy at St. Albans. (Since I've told Andy that I used to go to a boy's boarding school, I think that might have influenced this radical change in the story). Not content to have merely one expensive school, Gunderhold has established a second campus in Kaputo, an island half way between California and Hawaii that recently became America's 51st state. But Gunderhold has other secret, nefarious plans. (He always does). Attached to the school is a large, mysterious and heavily guarded laboratory. The occasional, inquisitive student is told that it's a research laboratory whose work will greatly benefit the school. And, in a sense, in the bizarre mind of Garret J. Gunderhold, it will. But Gunderhold's plans far exceed the school. His "stage" always encompasses nothing less than the world itself. This time his "genetic realignment" experiments involve his life-long obsession to create a man, indeed a race of people, born with wings and the capacity to fly. That dream may seem noble enough, but he wants to use his winged humans to conquer Rinaldia and other Crasian countries like Rudolfa and Rhodnesia. Who knows what he has in mind for the US?

. . . Today the sky was such a brilliant shade of blue I couldn't resist emptying the trash myself. (Usually my assistant/caretaker, a recent college graduate, does that.) It takes 19 strides, steps really, for me to reach the garbage cans. Almost immediately, I start wishing I was playing basketball or bodysurfing in the Pacific or just walking on this cool September day for a mile or so. I start working on myself, trying to convince myself that I can do it and finally I try but can only manage about 50 steps. Later, my legs throb with a sciatica-type pain for hours, paying me back for my foolishness.

. . . At night I have a strange dream. I'm following my father, at first through the large, labyrinth-like house I grew up in. Later, I follow him outdoors, in the backyard, then to a place I've never been to before. The grass is high and thick, the trees as thin as cigarettes, and the sky is a somber, dark blue. I'm walking fast, almost running, but can't quite catch up to my 65-year-old father. For some reason, I don't ask him to stop, perhaps because, though he doesn't turn around, I know he knows I'm behind him.

Then the grass turns into a field of wet weeds. The ground also has become wet and muddy. I want to talk now. I want to say some magical combination of words that will make him stop but instead continue to chase after him through the dark weeds in silence. Soon I start to hear violin music, which seems to make sense, since my father was a professional violinist, only I can see that he's not playing, that the poignant music appears to be coming from the lake just beyond us.

"Gofus, wake up."

"Sorry, Wad," I say, using the other nickname we have for each other.

"Why did you fall asleep, Wad? It's only 3:27 in the afternoon."

"It's because of the medicine I'm taking for my legs. Sometimes, it makes me tired."

"When are you going to get better, Gofus?" His shining brown eyes fix directly on mine.

"Soon I hope."

"Good, then you can stop limping around like a wad."

He looks closely at me for a second, checking to see if he inadvertently hurt my feelings. I have so many memories of swimming in pools, lakes and oceans with Andy, also of playing catch and wiffleball in our backyard, and of riding bikes to Forest Park, bowling, playing Hide and Seek or just walking, or traveling in general, especially in the summer. Last summer, because of my legs, we went nowhere though he traveled with his mother.

"Hey, Wad," Andy says, with a smile, "if you went to Gunderhold's lab you could get a pair of wings and fly."

"That would be a big improvement." I say, pointing to my legs. For a second, a serious look flashes across his face.

"What would you do if you had wings?" I say.

"I don't know. Gunderhold wants to use them to create an army of flying soldiers to annex countries for Wadovia."

"I know that. I meant what would you do, if you could fly?"

"I don't know, Wad. Let's go back to the story."

...That night I heard him repeatedly bouncing a ball in his room for over an hour. The next afternoon, after he got back from school, I insisted we play a game of indoor catch like we used to. We threw the wiffle ball standing five to ten feet apart in my living room for five minutes or so. It went alright but he said he wanted to stop and go back to telling the story. I am increasingly worried that he has no friends at school. I remember someone in a men's group telling me how he said to his 13-year-old son, "I want to be your friend just not your only friend."

...When Andy is with his mother, I have my worst times and my darkest thoughts. I'm alone much of that time yet rarely answer the phone or call anyone myself. My assistant shops for me and does some cleaning and other domestic chores. He's a young guy just out of college, but he seems wary of me and always keeps his distance.

. . . Yesterday, the sky was a cloudless blue and the air crisp and spring-like, though it is mid-October. I was alone (Andy was using the computer in his room) and against my doctor's orders, I couldn't resist sneaking out for a little walk again. I felt a little unsteady (my Gralise and Nucynta no doubt often contributes to this) as I went down the stairs of my condo in my stockinged feet. I moved slowly and still my fingers trembled as I held onto the railing. I stared at the sky, at the tall trees in my small backyard and at the pine and magnolia trees in my front yard. I saw the trees move in the wind. It was very beautiful. When I looked between the trees I saw Andy watching me through his window.

That night I dreamt I was watching my father while he was studying a musical score. In the middle of his life, he began conducting (in addition to being the first violinist in the orchestra). I walked a few steps closer and soon could hear him humming some of the music. I think it was a passage from a Mahler symphony. His arms began moving rhythmically as if he were conducting an invisible orchestra. It was something I'd seen many times, and never tired of watching, in my waking life. Later, I dreamed that I was chasing him up a mountain. Since I was so much younger, I should have been able to catch him but I never could, and soon he disappeared (as if he were flying) over the mountain top.

...From my window I can see some of the people from my street walking their kids to the same elementary school I used to walk Andy to. I usually try to look out that window around five to eight in the morning and then around three in the afternoon when they walk their kids back home. It makes me envious sometimes, but still I need to see it.

. . . As I said, my father had a philosophical kind of mind. Like me, he was baffled by the universe, but unlike me never gave up thinking about it. I remember one conversation with him that dealt with mans' attempts to have his work, or art, endure. "If the world ends, man's work won't be remembered, but if it doesn't end and time is infinite, it won't be remembered either."

"Not even Beethoven or Shakespeare?" I said.

"Not even them," he said.

Now that I can barely walk and my father

is dead I find myself thinking similar thoughts. My writing seems more vain and, in vain, than ever.

. . . Every night he was with me I used to kiss Andy goodnight on his forehead and say, "I love you" but he never said it back. That used to frustrate me (just as I used to be frustrated waiting for words I wanted to hear from certain women). I'm still able to reassure myself that he does love me, however. I've learned to go by his eyes.

Perhaps because neither my father nor my mother played sports with me (both were always playing their violins), I tried very hard to play sports with Andy, but he wasn't interested in any of them. The only thing he would play with me was wiffleball in our backyard and even then he would barely tolerate the hitting and mainly enjoyed our telling the story while we played catch. As far as I know, he never played sports with any kids from his school either. I guess the fact that he's a computer, indoors kinda kid has turned out to be a kind of lucky break for me now that the outdoors is basically something I only see through the windows. "The outdoors is so twentieth century," he once said to me.

Tonight, from Andy's room, where the door is always closed, I hear the constant sound of a bouncing ball again as I have for the last few weeks. It could just be a random compulsive activity like the long time he spends washing his hands, but I can't help thinking he's trying to communicate something to me—perhaps his frustration that I don't play outside with him anymore and because he sees how I "walk" is afraid to ask me.

"Hey Wad, wanna play catch outside with

me?" I say to him. I'm thinking I could do it if I had to for a few minutes.

"No thanks, Gofus. I'm still using the computer."

"But Wad, it's beautiful outside. There's not a cloud in the sky. Come on."

"Don't be such a Gunderhold about it, Wad."

"I just don't want you to be bored."

"I'm fine, Gofus." And that's that.

...The only time when I can move freely without pain is in my dreams. Too often, however, the medications I take mask or simply obliterate them and, if they even occurred, they're difficult to remember. Though I'm sleeping more than I ever have as an adult I've gone a week without remembering a single dream. It feels like I've metamorphosed into some kind of plant or barnacle. Meanwhile, Andy's had to wake me up the last two mornings.

"Wad, I'm up," he'll say, which means it's time to bring him his orange juice and breakfast before he goes to school. It's odd, or maybe not, that he never asks to help in spite of seeing how I walk, though it's also true he'll do whatever I ask with only minor complaining. Andy has always hated talking about painful things and can't even bear to describe a death or serious injury that takes place in our stories.

. . . When I don't dream, I turn to memories, though no sexual ones. It's too painful to think of that lost world in which in my own hideous quest for "power" I often behaved like a Gunderhold. I'm especially fond of remembering my last vacation with Andy when we ran along St. Petersburg Beach and swam in the warm water underneath the Florida sun. (I was only feeling intermittent pain then). It was maybe the last time I was more like a father and less like the grandfather kind of figure I've become since I lost my mobility.

Last summer all he did when he was with me was tell stories and watch DVDs of old TV shows like *Seinfeld* or *Columbo* or movies like *Napolian Dynamite* or *The Birds*—although there is no movie like *The Birds*. Yet he acted like that was enough for him...

. . . It's impossible for an invalid not to start doing some magical thinking. What caused my condition (perhaps when Pest Control sprayed my place for bugs), what could cure it—perhaps supplements like ALA or Turmeric. My "belief" that memory, dreams and the story with Andy, can somehow provide a replacement world or at least a shelter from the reality of my invalid world may be a form of magical thinking, too.

. . . Had a memory of Andy last night that made me laugh in my bed. When he was about four, we used to sometimes take baths together. One time in the tub, he stared at his penis and said with all earnestness "Does it fall off?" I said no but wanted to add, "Not if you meet the right woman."

. . . Today I saw him staring at me as I slowly got up from the couch to go to the bathroom. At night he began bouncing his tennis ball again at a furious pace. I managed to get out of bed more quickly than usual to say, "Hey, Andy, what's up?"

"Nothing, Gofus." Then he opened the door. "Oh, by the way, Wad, Gunderhold got his wings and flew away."

"Really?"

"Yeah, Gunderhold is dead."

. . . This afternoon, before my Nucynta and Gralise kicked in and made me too dizzy, I slowly walked outside a few steps, again. The wind was blowing through the trees. I only stayed out a minute at most but I touched the magnolia leaves and the pine needles from the tree next to it.

. . . That day I finally remembered my dream. I was in the Berkshires walking through the grove that leads to Lake Mahkeenac with my father and Andy. We were all joking and laughing although I can't remember what any of the jokes were. We were in our bathing suits and proceeded to walk into the lake where we soon began playing catch with a brightly colored ball. Everyone was smiling while we played waist deep in the water. Andy was smiling from ear to ear. I thought, now, at last, he has a new friend. Then my father said we should all swim out to the raft, which was odd because the water there was over our heads and my father didn't know how to swim. But somehow we all made it out to the raft. We sat down and looked at the hills that surrounded the lake and at the sail boats with their white sails. When I turned to look at my father again he was gone and I was alone on the raft with Andy.

I woke up expecting it to be night and to be alone in my room but instead there was still light out, and I was on the couch in the family room where Andy was watching me.

"Hey, Wad, want to tell the story?"

"Sure, Gofus," he said and soon began running through the living room to the door and back. I thought maybe it's okay, even if parts of the world start to slip away, if you have a son running back and forth with his arms in the air like wings, laughing the whole time until you, too, inevitably laugh.

THE ENDLESS VISIT

Incredible how easily she fell in with him, let him have his way with her. Too horrible to think it was because of his money or that money was even a primary factor, but what else could she think? She knew she was attractive or attractive enough not to have to have an affair with someone twice her age, so what else could it be? Besides, she'd already accepted a number of gifts from him, and now Walter was talking about taking her to Rome and Switzerland. Worse still, lately she'd been fantasizing about his money while they made love and worrying that he somehow knew it. It was irrational to think he could know her thoughts, but she worried anyway. Walter was a clever man who couldn't be fooled for long. He'd made his money in banking and the stock market—had inherited some from one parent and was waiting for the rest from another. It was ghoulish, his waiting around for death to happen so he could get still more money, yet there she was sleeping with him—a man as old as her father (assuming her father, wherever he was, was still alive)—so wasn't she as bad or worse than Walter or for that matter Barbara, who in essence was doing the same thing herself? Barbara was, in fact, looking steadily at her now, staring at her with huge blue eyes a hypnotist would kill for. It took Carla a few seconds to realize Barbara had come to one of her rare rest stops and was waiting for her to say something.

"You knew what it would be like. Whenever you see her it's always the same," Carla finally said.

"No, this time it was different."

"How? How was it different?"

"This time it was just incredible—It was like no time had gone by at all since the last time I went to Florida. Like it was all part of the same endless visit."

"Okay, so you want to tell me?" Carla said, running her fingers through her hair. It was long and dark (the approximate color of Barbara's) and hung down straight below her waist. Barbara did the same thing a moment later to her own hair.

"If you don't want me to or—"

"No, no. Go ahead—"

Barbara smiled for a second, then closed her eyes and drew in a breath (while Carla quickly checked her watch). They were sitting on facing chairs a few feet apart at the far end of Barbara's loft. Her finished paintings and paintings-in-progress were hung all around them. Garish, melodramatic abstracts that looked like dismembered animals or worse, as far as Carla was concerned.

"This time she not only turned me down cold about the money—even though it's nearly Christmas—I expected that, but this time there wasn't even a pretense of any interest in me."

"That's par for the course," Carla said.

"No, no, I usually get a pretense, but this time nothing at all about my life, nothing about my paintings either, of course. Yet she had obviously spent an absurd amount of time on her makeup to impress me. When I commented on how nice her living room looked she said, 'I still think all my best assets are above my neck, don't you?' as if she were afraid I was calculating the worth of her adored antiques that were crowded all around us. 'I still have all my own teeth,' she said, 'I have very few wrinkles—just a few around my mouth and none on my forehead and look at my hair—at my age, most women's hair begins to get thinner, but mine is getting thicker and longer.'"

"She moved forward a bit in her chair the better to show me her face. I sat forward too and stared at my mother. It was funny, but despite the painted-on look of her hard, red lipstick and her marmalade-orange rouge, the total effect wasn't bad—made her look as if she really had tricked time and really would always look pretty and never too old."

"It sounds like you're hallucinating her instead of seeing her," Carla said.

"No, no, I hallucinate nothing—I see her all too clearly. Believe me. It wouldn't be the same every time if I didn't see her clearly."

"Okay, okay. It was just a thought—so, go on," Carla said.

Another little intake of air like a fish and Barbara continued. It was not going to be a good listening day, Carla thought. As soon as she heard "Florida . . . mother . . . painting" she felt like saying, "I'm experiencing my own déjà vu here, Barbara, my own endless visit. Is the purpose of my life to listen to your same story after I've already spent the whole day working for you?" But, of course, she said nothing and kept trying to look interested.

People always assumed she was a good listener but why? Maybe it was just the look on her face, just something a little pale or unaggressive about her. Because speech was, like everything else, about aggression. You talked because you talked first. You got the power of talking because you seized it. It was the contemporary version of the western gun duel. Whoever drew first and shot killed the other with their speech—only it was a slow death through repeated verbal assault. And people didn't just talk, they confessed. They told her about their incest and drug addiction and fantasies about children and, in Barbara's case, her unrecognized artistic brilliance and her hatred for her mother, the narcissistic miser. Then the last few months also about Joan, the latest young lover to have left her, and then on to the entire ontology of her lesbianism.

There was supposed to be a passive power in listening, but Carla never felt it. Instead it was like playing Ping-Pong with your hands strapped behind your back. It was a constant attack during which you could do nothing as the words kept hitting you one after another like Ping-Pong balls. Where was the power in that?

It was the same with Walter. They were at the bar in SoHo, he was a nice-looking man, but much older. Yet somehow he dared to start talking—drew his gun first, as it were, and it was all over. Not just for that night but for their whole relationship. The pattern had been set and that was it. If there were going to be any deviations from it, any surprises, he would provide them. And so he did, although they were always below the waist surprises. Things he would do to her, things involving his below the waist life. But she was never surprised above the waist—in her mind—by him or Barbara either. When would she, Carla, surprise someone else? What was keeping her from interrupting Barbara and saying, "Enough said, Boss. I've got to be going now." Or maybe something a little less direct but ultimately leaving, at least, or deciding when she would leave so she could attend to her own life where Walter was waiting for her. If only there were some way to make Barbara stop or just disappear but Carla had great difficulty interrupting her, or Walter either, just like she had trouble interrupting her own mother when she was alive or even talking to her own father before he left for the west. She thought about him disappearing into California like a termite inside a house and shuddered.

"My mother found a new obsession!" she heard Barbara say. It was as if her volume button had suddenly been pressed, as if she were somehow part human, part T.V.

"It was early, yet she wanted to take me to dinner to 'a classy new restaurant' in Gulfport near the pier," Barbara continued. "Since she'd never spent more than eight dollars on me for any meal, my curiosity was piqued. First, as a kind of hors d'oeuvre, she wanted to show me her condominium clubhouse (which, of course, she'd already shown me several times before) where my father used to play bridge, then the streets of her beloved Gulfport.

We walked along the sidewalk parallel to the town beach. My mother told me for the umpteenth time about how my father loved to walk down this sidewalk with his shirt open. She invariably talked to me about him as if she were describing a very important man I barely knew, as if I hadn't grown up with him and seen and known his habits for myself. I admit the man jumped to fulfill her every whim, but I'd still had my own relationship with him, hadn't I?

We walked onto the main street of the town littered with pseudo art galleries and junky stores—places called 'Top This Boutique' and 'Van Gogh's Art Gallery.' Of course my mother said it was all charming and elegant and asked several times to go to the art galleries but I said no. She'd never once gone to New York to see any galleries with me despite my many invitations, much less ever visited my loft to see my paintings. When it came to my work, she only saw the paintings I'd give her as presents, all of which she more or less hid in her home. Actually, my mother had never visited me once since I moved to New York. She always got me to visit her where she could set the agenda simply because she'd paid the fare. Wait," Barbara said, taking a deep breath. "I need to slow down. I can hear myself whining like a monster."

"It's okay. You don't need to go on if you don't want to," Carla said.

"I just want to tell you about our lunch at the great La Cote Basque," Barbara said sarcastically, "the town's most pretentious restaurant. That's where it all happened. From the outside it's ambiguous looking, a white one story with a wine-red, sloping roof. It could be anything without its big red sign to tell you otherwise—a local museum, a whorehouse—anything. You step inside and it's so nonsensically dark, you feel like you've literally gone underground. The candles are just strong enough to see the absurd Christmas colors that dominate the place—fake roses everywhere and cheap white lace and a stucco ceiling with hideous, fake-green plants and baskets of plastic fruit dangling from it like rows of sagging breasts. Except for the walls, filled with bad copies of impressionist paintings, you'd think you were in someone's basement or fallout shelter. 'My God, I'm in Wayne's World,

I thought, as I was ushered to my seat by a waiter in a ridiculously tight tuxedo. Around us in the half-filled room were a series of soon-to-be corpses dining serenely. I looked at the menu beside the pseudo-silver place mats and then I understood my mother's urgency in getting there. It was still early enough for us to qualify for the Early Bird Special. I scanned the prices: the most expensive dish was a roast lamb for $7.95—at least it was $7.95 until 5:30 in the afternoon and it was only 5:07, so her streak would stay intact."

"How much money did you say your mother was worth?"

"Over two million in her Solomon Brothers account alone. Who knows what she has in the bank? And almost all of it because of what my father gave her, not that he ever knew how stingy she'd be with me. Anyway, I was eating my utterly tasteless Early Bird Special, certainly not planning any kind of confrontation when she starts complaining about how she'd like a grandchild and I'm thinking, 'You don't even pay attention to me and I'm your only child, why would you want another person to ignore?' except I knew the answer to that—it would be something else she could brag about to her condominium neighbors while she sat around the pool. Of course she'd nagged me about not having a child hundreds of times before, but I mean, I'm 38 now, I'd officially come out to her the year before, even written her a long letter about sleeping with Joan, among other things. Does she not only not listen to me but also not read or remember my letters either? Still she hadn't said any ultra provocative thing yet. I mean, I was used to the grandchild remarks. Instead, she went on flitting from one area of conversation to another (her health, her money worries, her nosy neighbors), and I really believed I was going to make it without exploding when, apropos of nothing, she suddenly said, 'Are you still painting, Barbara?' She may as well have said, 'Are you still breathing?' She may as well have said, 'Who are you? I've heard a rumor you're alive.' Something broke in me then. It was like I didn't really exist, like I had suddenly disappeared and there was nothing but air where my body should have been."

Carla kept her eyes on Barbara but stopped listening. Walter was already in her apartment by now. She had her own melodrama to worry about. She'd even thought of interrupting Barbara and telling her a bit of her own story, 'I've got a 54-year-old boyfriend waiting in my apartment with a Viagra erection' could be her opening line. 'So I've got a limited amount of time to get home, capice? I mean I really have to be leaving now.' But once Barbara got going on one of her monologues it seemed impossible to stop her, and she'd already stayed almost 15 minutes past the end of her workday. Even if Barbara gave her a little extra or paid for a cab, it just wasn't fair. If she was going to be treated like an in-house therapist (always potentially on-call) she should be paid like one. She shouldn't have to also do the secretarial stuff, too. She could feel herself starting to get angry. What, after all, was the big crisis here? Yes, it was sad that Joan dumped her, sadder still that Barbara kept chasing girls who were too young, but everyone gets dumped and was it any sadder than her pathetic situation with Walter? As for the money, Barbara knew she'd eventually inherit it, which was more than Carla could look forward to. Although she was 11 years younger than Barbara, Carla was already a de facto orphan. So what was the great tragedy here? That because she couldn't get the loan she wanted from her mother, Barbara had to teach a class or two in a prep school and couldn't devote all her time to her deluded painting career? Was the tragedy that she still had to teach? Didn't Barbara have her Carla to do her filing and type her letters and listen to her stories? She would never have any of that. The only way she could afford a loft like Barbara's was—Walter, who was waiting with his penis up in the air until it would finally pirouette down to earth in the very near future. She'd really have to interrupt soon. But what was this? Barbara Boss was crying now, had a veritable orgasm of self-pity, her face already wet with tears.

"Are you okay?" Carla said, surprising herself by putting a hand on Barbara's shoulder. Barbara nodded while sobbing softly.

"You sure you're alright?"

"I'm okay," Barbara said, blowing her nose noisily. "I'll be right back, I've got to pee." She watched Barbara get up and leave for the bathroom. She was glad she'd touched Barbara's shoulder and acted nice. It seemed when she acted nice she felt less angry. She didn't really like it when she thought dark thoughts about Barbara, called her "Barbara Boss" or worse to herself. Besides, in any long-term sense, Barbara wasn't really the problem. If she weren't Barbara's servant, it would be somebody else, wouldn't it? Never had she been able to do anything but servile work for others. She had tried to be a photographer, but if she were really honest with herself, the trying had been mostly in her mind. She'd left art school, then community college after a year, and every relationship as soon as the possibility of living with someone presented itself. On the one hand, she kept getting involved with men but they all disappointed her or made her angry and eventually either she or they were unfaithful. She was faithful only as a servant, it seemed. She was faithful to Barbara, worked for her, and listened to her resentfully after hours and also felt uncomfortable because of the lesbian thing, sometimes very uncomfortable, though Barbara's occasional passes were ambiguous, never overt.

Carla got up from her chair and walked toward the bathroom. It occurred to her that there were razors and sleeping pills in there. She also knew that Barbara (who'd been robbed once and mugged twice) kept a gun in the closet by the bathroom. Barbara had actually told her where it was. Should she check to see if it was still there? She suddenly felt a great anxiety that she hadn't listened more carefully to Barbara and, as if to compensate, placed her ear to the door and listened as closely as she could. All she could hear was Barbara peeing, as if her stream of urine was the only sound left in the world. It was odd to be listening to something like that and odder still that again it made her feel sorry for her. Then the door suddenly opened—Carla was barely able to avoid being hit in the face by it.

"Hi," Barbara said, looking surprised of course.

"Hi," was all Carla could manage.

"I'm sorry for all the histrionics."

"I was worried about you. That's why I sort of followed you."

Barbara squeezed Carla's hands for a second. "Thanks for worrying. I've got a perfect solution for both of us," she said, walking into the kitchen part of the loft. Carla followed behind her looking at her watch.

"Can you hold these?" Barbara said, handing her two glasses. "I'll take the vodka and tonic. We can drink it in our chairs."

As soon as they sat down Barbara said, "I really am sorry that I broke down. Breakdowns suck."

"Don't worry about it," Carla said, gesturing with her free hand. "I'm really sorry this happened to you—again."

"In all of the world, you're the only one."

"What?" Carla said.

"Who's sorry—for me. Who listens to me. Not even my shrink listens like that and she charges $200 an hour—so will you have one drink with me?"

"Sure. Okay. I'm gonna drink it kind of quickly, though."

"The better to get to the next one," Barbara said, laughing.

They clinked glasses and finished nearly half their drinks in one swallow. Carla liked the buzz and finished the rest of hers as if it were lemonade.

"Seriously, you're an extraordinarily sensitive person, you are," Barbara said, pouring her another drink. Carla was oddly moved by the compliment, especially coming from Barbara, who was so reluctant to give them generally. Yet there was something unsettling about it, too. Also unsettling was the image of Walter in the back of her brain, like a stalled oarsman in a boat race trying to move forward, so she took her second drink and finished it almost as quickly as the first.

More tributes followed from Barbara. She was talking and drinking fast and continuing to look at her steadily. "It's meant so much to me to have you here these last few months. To have someone to talk to like you. I, I don't ever think of you as an 'employee,' you know, I really always think of you as my friend."

Carla looked down at the floor, feeling vaguely nervous, but there was nothing there to look at so she raised her head again. Barbara was still looking right at her.

"I know I've become kind of dependent on you lately—especially since Joan left. I know I've been talking a lot. I hope I'm not taking advantage."

Carla made a little inadvertent shrug, mumbled, "No," then held out her glass, which Barbara filled quickly.

"I just want you to know that I do appreciate you. I do. I think I'd do almost anything for you because you're such a fine, feeling person. I also think it's so incredibly unusual that such a beautiful gift is inside such an attractive package."

Carla took another swallow and tried to unravel the metaphor. Her soul was the gift she supposed and the package would be her face and her body. Yes, that was quite a compliment—maybe the best she'd ever gotten—a genuine above-the-waist surprise. 'Thank you," she said.

"Can I just give you a hug for all that you've done today and all the other days?"

Carla stood up to receive the hug. How could she refuse to hug her boss? Barbara held her tightly, trembling with emotion. "Carla, I don't know what I'd do without you."

So, I'm being hugged and kissed now. What's next? Carla thought. It felt basically the same as when Walter kissed and touched her so why make a fuss?

"Should I stop now?" Barbara whispered in her ear. Carla found that she couldn't speak.

Incredible how easily it all happened then, how easy it was for Barbara to take her by the hand and lead her to her bedroom complimenting her the whole way, a-mile-a-minute. And then the undressing, the unusual yet all too usual orders, and everything else. Even while it was going on, she tried to understand the reasons why she was letting it happen. There was the alcohol, of course, her anger at Walter, and also, more than anything, some inner desire to do something radical, outrageous.

When it was over she turned away because she didn't want Barbara to see her face or to kiss her and call her "baby" or anything like that. For once, Barbara seemed to understand her feelings or else wanted the same thing herself, which wouldn't be surprising. She knew Barbara's type—lots of surface emotion and neediness but not much interest in giving too long to someone else. Whatever it was, Carla got away with just a couple of quick hand squeezes.

"What a day!" Barbara said, propping her head up with her pillows.

"Really," Carla said.

"Well, you were certainly the best part of it."

"Thanks," Carla said. She would not, no matter what, compliment her back. She'd done enough for the woman already, goddamn it.

"So, tell me what you're feeling? Are you surprised?"

"Kind of."

Barbara gave a little laugh. "Was it— different? I mean, this was your first time with a woman, right?"

"Yes," Carla said, turning to face her with what she hoped was a Mona Lisa-type smile. Finally she said what she knew Barbara wanted to hear but felt angry for saying it. It wasn't even true; it had actually been kind of like being with Walter—like eating food without much taste. But why should sex really be any different with a woman (or at least with this woman) just because the female dictator had a different set of genitals?

There was an uncomfortable silence until Barbara finally said, "I'm feeling like I've been really selfish keeping you so long, and you've just been too kind to say so."

"I should make a call."

"Of course, I've kept you too long—though I can't deny I'm really glad I did," Barbara said with a smile, followed by another hand squeeze. "Can you just wait a minute? I want to give you something before you go."

"Sure," Carla said. Barbara put on her panties as she got out of bed but walked through her loft bare-chested, her large breasts already sagging like a middle-aged woman's, Carla thought. She quickly put on her own underclothes thinking that Barbara would maybe give her a nice sweater or else a bottle of perfume. It was good that she realized she'd have to give something, that she'd just had her last free one. In the future, if this happened again, she would have to pay in cash, and not $25 either, but $50 or maybe $100—she knew Barbara had it, no matter how much she complained. She had a bathtub of fifties.

Just before Barbara returned, she picked a sentence to use to say thank you. Barbara was walking towards her from the far corner of the loft carrying something big. Without her glasses Carla couldn't tell what it was but didn't want Barbara to see her wearing them. Then the sun started to come in through the main window, lighting Barbara up for a few seconds like some kind of illuminated angel. The next thing she knew Barbara—all smiles now—was handing her one of her abstracts filled with loud, swirling, vomitous colors. The painting was four or five feet high.

"For you," Barbara said, handing the painting to Carla, who didn't even want to be near it, much less touch it. She felt tricked but still managed to smile and say the thank-you sentence she'd practiced.

"This is one of the first paintings I did in this loft, so I'm a little sentimental about it," Barbara said, with her blue eyes glowing. "But I think it still holds up, and I really want you to have it. It's called 'Oval Romance.'"

It's called eating someone for nothing, Carla thought, but still was able to say something nice about the painting and then sincerely thanked Barbara for the canvas cover that she slipped over it. At least no one would see her carrying it. Now it was just some big, mysterious clumsy thing that she hoped could fit in her cab.

"Christ," Barbara said. "I can't believe I have to pee again. It must be something you do to me— excite all my bodily fluids," she said, touching Carla's cheek and laughing. Carla forced a smile. "Why don't you make your call while I'm in the bathroom and then I'll say goodbye," Barbara said as she left the room.

Carla looked at the phone by the bed but wasn't tempted. It was too late to call Walter now and offer any normal excuse, and she didn't have the energy to tell him a preposterous health emergency or death-in-the-family type lie. Besides, what was Walter? Just another boss, like Barbara. Maybe, since it had to end anyway, she wouldn't call at all, either that or tell the outrageous lie later. She only knew she couldn't see him or call him right now. Everything had somehow become different. The only thing that was the same was the anger she was feeling for not having left Barbara earlier, for enduring the whole thing, especially going to bed with Barbara—where she'd acted like Barbara's slave with the additional, almost certain result that she'd ruined her job. Because now it would either turn her into a prostitute, if Barbara were willing to pay, or if she refused Barbara, she'd probably be fired and sooner rather than later—which would make her need Walter again. Impossible not to hate Barbara then for getting her half-drunk and tricking her into bed where she'd humiliated her and then, the final insult of that hideous painting.

She sat down on the bed, closed her eyes, and tried to think it all out of existence. There were times, once a long stretch of time earlier in the day when Barbara was talking, when Carla hadn't heard a word she'd said. If you concentrated well enough you could do amazing things with your mind, even select what you heard or saw—at least, she could. So that now, while she went to the closet in the hallway, took the gun and walked into the bathroom where Barbara was flushing the toilet, she focused completely on a childhood walk by a stream she took with her father. Just the two of them—one of the few vivid memories she had of him. That vision lasted till she fired the gun and even then she managed to see nothing—maybe just a split second of Barbara's face which she instantly erased. Then, for a while, she didn't know where she was.

. . . When she returned to the present she started putting on her clothes quickly, otherwise she worried that when Barbara returned she might think she wanted a second round. Where was Barbara anyway? When Carla looked at her watch she was shocked at how much time had passed and decided to walk toward the bathroom and ask what was going on. Perhaps she could simply say good-bye from the other side of the door. She knocked and said, "Barbara," but got no answer. "Barbara, are you all right?" she said two more times. She tried the door, which was unlocked, and walked into the bathroom. She didn't see the body that was lying between the toilet and the shower. Instead she walked out into the loft, calling her name more loudly. It was not a large loft and her normal voice could easily be heard from any part of it, but she was yelling anyway as she quickly circled the floor, opening what few doors there were to try to find her.

She went back to the bathroom—looked in the bathtub in case Barbara were playing some kind of erotic game and was hiding there—but didn't find her. It was ridiculous, Carla thought. It wasn't as if you could lose track of a person like misplacing a key. She looked out the bathroom window—there was no fire escape near it, nothing at all which Barbara would have used. She looked down again but saw nothing on the sidewalk, though if Barbara had jumped the police or ambulance would certainly have been there by now.

She circled the loft once more, trying to grasp what had happened. It wasn't as if she had fallen asleep—she definitely hadn't—so Barbara couldn't have left the bathroom, much less the loft, without her hearing. Besides, Barbara was half-naked when she went to the bathroom, was carrying no clothes, and definitely hadn't returned to the bedroom. But this was an absurd line of speculation since she definitely would have heard the bathroom door opening, not to mention the heavy main door to the loft, which was still bolted with that extra deadbolt lock that could only be used from the inside. Carla looked at that small table in the hallway and saw that the apartment keys were still on it.

She felt herself go lightheaded as she walked through the loft again but told herself it was important not to panic, that it would interfere with her concentration. Yet she felt ridiculous as she stared preternaturally hard without blinking, as if she were looking for an ant instead of a person.

At the end of her next circle, she saw the

gun on the floor near the bathroom door. At first she was startled, horrified, but she was sure it hadn't been fired or else, of course, she would have heard it. It was probably dislodged somehow without her realizing it when she'd opened the closet door the first time Barbara had gone to the bathroom. She decided not to touch it. If she or someone else eventually had to call the police it would be better not to have touched it. Though who would call about poor Barbara? Her self-absorbed mother might not call for weeks—and Joan, her last girlfriend, had long ago left her. It was December now, Christmas vacation at Barbara's school, which wouldn't open again for a month.

She didn't know how much time passed before her attitude about Barbara's disappearance began to change. First her watch suddenly seemed as useless to her as a mole, and she stopped looking at it or even being aware of it. Then her head started to hurt and she found herself walking back to the bedroom. She lay down on the bed thinking about other explanations for the disappearance. Words from Barbara's conversation came back to her.

Hadn't she said, after her mother asked if she were still painting, that she felt as if she'd disappeared? Simply replaced by empty space. Could Barbara have somehow willed this?

Her headache began to subside. It was perhaps irrational to think that way, but the fact was Barbara had disappeared, and it had to have happened somehow. Better, perhaps, to accept the disappearance and deal with its consequences than to try and explain it. What was life, after all, but accepting one improbability after another? You accepted that you were your parents' child, that you were a woman and had to act like one. You accepted your consciousness as if it were the air you breathed, and then you accepted your death, your eventual disappearance and the disappearance of everything else. Your own personal endless visit from death.

Carla felt herself shudder and closed her eyes again. When she opened them it was because the sun had come out once more and lit up the room, which seemed to make her mood brighter as well. She felt herself smile. With Barbara's disappearance she was now free to leave the loft, but in light of her decision about Walter, there was suddenly no reason to leave right away. Why not see what it felt like to be rich and stay in a nice place for awhile? When she would leave, she thought she should probably take the gun with her and get rid of it. She was sure of that. But at least she wouldn't have to take that atrocious painting with her. That was a relief and a victory of sorts. As for deciding anything else, there was really no reason now to rush.

FLAME

Once more I told the man behind the counter at St. Louis Bread Company (who has only waited on me a handful of times in the last few years) that he has an excellent memory when he called me by my correct first name. He smiled such a beaming, angelic smile you'd think it was Christmas morning and he was eight years old. It will be the happiest I'll make anybody today, I thought wistfully.

I had just come from the UPS store where Simone works. Despite her name, Simone looks exactly like a young Simon to me (about the same age as the counter man at the Bread Company and almost as masculine). However, Simone is almost certainly a work in progress. There are still no signs of breasts beneath her black UPS uniform shirt, and her face and short hair make her look like a young man. Yet, last time I noticed how hairless her arms are. For someone with medium-brown hair this almost certainly means that they were shaved. I thought of my father's proverb "great distances begin with small steps." How he would loathe what I'm doing. I hadn't even told him I'd left my job (he's a man who'd rather die than stop working), much less anything about Simone.

Whenever I'm in the store, it's difficult to keep my eyes off Simone. I'm always mildly disturbed by this but continue to watch her as much as I can without her realizing it. I know this is maddeningly bourgeois, even vulgar behavior, yet I can't seem to stop it. It's become one of the ways I continue to disappoint myself.

Finally, I left the UPS store and went to Walgreens, which is just off the mall. There are a number of people I look at there, plus the cashier nearest the door always welcomes me in a friendly way. She has a smile worth preserving, too, though not in the way Simone's is. One might wonder how I have the time to go to so many stores in the middle of the day, in the middle of the week? It's because I retired—much earlier than I should have perhaps or so my colleagues at the office kept telling me. But I did it because it was what I always told myself I'd do if I ever got any money and so when the money came, it was as if it were expected of me. Maybe if I'd enjoyed the office, or the company of my coworkers, I wouldn't have left so suddenly, but it had reached the point (some time ago actually) where it was a burden to even pretend to care about them. My smiles in the office were definitely not worth preserving, neither was anything I said or did. I was little more than a worker zombie numbly moving through my programmed day. If I must be reduced to a monster, let me be a vampire instead—society's latest monster of choice, that it seems endlessly fascinated by. Vampires are everything zombies aren't—sleek, aggressive, dangerously attractive, compelling. Too much to aspire to probably, but then again, I'd never know unless I retired. As long as I work in an office like mine, I thought, I'm doomed to be an uninteresting lethargic monster, simply taking up space.

I dreamed about Simone's arms last night. I was looking at them in the UPS store, but this time she saw what I was doing and showed me a smile of great mystery. The next thing I knew we were in one of the rooms of my parent's house. Then I woke up, walked into the living room, lit a candle, and stared long and hard at the flame. My finger was very close to the flame, but I didn't burn it.

I washed myself very thoroughly that morning while I wondered where I would go during my morning hours, which are usually the most difficult ones to get through unless one also counts the afternoon. In my private sense of justice, I think if you can get through a morning you ought to get credit for the afternoon, too. Since I rarely drive except when there's an emergency—I just became too anxious about it—my options are sometimes quite limited. Really this would be an ideal time to read but my interest in reading has also mysteriously evaporated these last few years. After a while, you tire of reading about humanity and you want to interact with it in a way that produces some change, if only in one or two people (although of all the people I know, only Simone is really trying to change).

I still have my love of music because it alone (except for some very great paintings) can express what is otherwise inexpressible in life and yet I have to be careful not to listen too often because it stirs up emotions that are better left alone. I mean memories of my childhood, so full of secrets, (though I've always had secrets and sometimes think I can't relax without one) and memories of my lost loves—generally lost because I ruined them. Sometimes I think the money is like reparations for all the relationships I've ruined. Paradoxical thinking, I know, but one can't always control one's thoughts.

That night I spent almost an hour staring at the candle again, feeling its heat near the tips of my fingers.

"Can I help you, sir?"

"Do you want to waive the signature?"

"Oh, I'm sorry, sir. What it means is, do you want to leave the package at the premises if there is no one there to sign for it?"

"Is it a business or residence?"

"No, sir. My shift ends at five o'clock, but the store stays open till seven."

These were the precious words my Simone said to me this week.

Did I question what I was doing? Of course I did, but I felt driven by a vision, as I hadn't been for a long time, which made me feel young again in a way that was ultimately irresistible.

Probably because we only talked in short spurts in the UPS store, our conversation never transcended the mundane. Yet, that was quite enough to provide those ineffable glimpses into her nature (her slightly forced pleasantness, for instance, with its attendant hinting at her secret pain, that alternated with her surprisingly confident presentation of self—as if she'd just gotten an "A" in a public speaking course. I also made a point of finding reasons to stay in the store where I could overhear her talking with other customers. I was surprised to discover how much I resented them. Once, I even heard a private conversation on her cell phone. I was completely blindsided! That there were people in her life, friends, perhaps even a lover who could call her at work and succeed in getting her to talk to them was...infuriating! It upset me so much that I couldn't really hear what she was saying, only snippets of it. Yet this fragmented, in many ways, horrifying experience ended up contributing to my general state of knowledge about her. It also made me understand that for there to be any progress in whatever I was pursuing I needed to see her outside her office. In fact, I needed to somehow see her in my home.

It's odd, in a mostly positive way, how we can respond to others, to life in general, in a fresh way once we're suddenly excited by just one person. Immediately after realizing I wanted to get Simone to come to my condominium, I called Scrubby Dutch to thoroughly clean it. Scrubby Dutch sends a cleaning crew of three women who work for an hour in exchange for fifty dollars. Because they clean everywhere, they wear faded jeans and old shirts. In short, they look like homeless women. I tried to stay out of their way in my computer room where I was monitoring my investments when I heard one of the doors from the adjoining bathroom shut. It was open just long enough for me to see which one of the three it was—the worst dressed one with dark-brown, scraggily hair. I stopped my work and listened to her pee. My close proximity obviously didn't inhibit her flow of urine. To my surprise,

I soon got aroused, which I immediately realized stemmed from my fascination with Simone and my plans for her. That was how my brain worked in those days.

What do people do with money when it comes so suddenly it's as if the wind blew it their way? I was lucky—mine came from a trust fund while my parents were still alive. Most people get theirs blown in by the winds of death. I was thinking these rather heavy thoughts in my bed somewhere between three and four in the morning—having conceded another victory to my indefatigably persistent insomnia.

Okay, I thought, people travel. At first, a celebratory trip to Europe or at least to Las Vegas. But I had become too anxious to travel just about the time my money arrived. Then they buy a house—perhaps the house of their dreams— but I dreaded few things more than shopping for a home and all that it involves with real estate agents and banks (I did, however, slightly upgrade my condominium). Then the suddenly rich get a financial advisor and start to plan how to make more money, but by nature, I'm not really equipped to trust financial advisors. For better or worse, I handle my own investments myself.

Instead of taking a grand vacation or buying a grand home or car or financial advisor, I used my money to retire. You're way too young to retire everyone said, but I did it anyway and haven't regretted it so far—though admittedly it's been less than a half year since I willingly joined the ranks of the unemployed. I'm aware, however, that there's a certain emptiness of purpose in my current way of living or was until I discovered Simone and realized very quickly after I began to focus on the situation that my number one asset (besides a kind of cunning intelligence) was the money I now had. The challenge was in the details, which made me realize I needed to do more research.

Back to the UPS store I went, always making sure Simone waited on me, that I had a bonafide question to ask, and that if any opportunity arose I could ask her a question about her life, even it if involved something as banal as asking where she lived or how she got to work, so I could possibly offer her a ride home. I was sufficiently older (and a long-time trusted customer) that her suspicion level seemed minimal. I didn't think she'd notice, for example, that I often showed up close to the time when her shift ended. That was the essence and beauty of her innocence.

You have a pair of eyes, but you don't know what to do with them. You don't want to look behind yourself because there's so much shame and disappointment in your past. You need to look ahead, but you need someone or something to make you do it. You can't help what that is—it selects you.

It was 5:03 when Simone came out of the store, and I was there to greet her.

"Good afternoon, sir," she said with her typical, trained politeness.

"Hi, Simone. Please call me Phillip."

"I'm sorry, Phillip," she said, nearly blushing. I noticed that her teeth were even whiter than her arms.

"Simone, can I talk with you for just a minute?"

"Yes, sir, Phillip," she said, as if covering all her bases. She stopped talking then and looked at me with her hopeful hazel blue eyes without asking what it was about, as if her manners had suddenly seized total control of the situation.

"Simone, you know my work makes me go to the UPS store a lot."

She nodded, eyes still on me.

"Well, during those visits I couldn't help observing how well you handle customers and your job in general. You prepare packages efficiently and skillfully, you fix the Xerox machines better than anyone else in the store, you use the computer knowledgably, and you type accurately and quickly. In short, you have a lot of impressive skills."

"Thank you, sir," she said, definitely blushing now.

"No, no, call me Phillip or Phil. I don't know anyone named 'sir'."

"Sorry, Phillip."

"That's better," I said. "Well, it so happens, as it often does because I always pick good people, that my special assistant has just accepted a job with a Chicago-based corporation that pays more than I can and reluctantly, tearfully," (I decided to add, being a sucker for the hyperbolic touch), "she had to leave just before I could complete an important project I'd been working on. Simone, what I'm hoping is that you might be interested in helping me finish it as my temporary, special assistant."

"Me?" she said, jabbing her titless chest just below her nametag with one of her impeccably manicured fingers.

"But I have my job at UPS."

"It won't interfere with that. I just need your help now for a little while. You can do the work at my office after your work at UPS ends, say an hour or two per day for a week or so and I'll triple what they pay you at UPS."

"Really? I just hope I have the ability to..."

"You have the ability," I said in my best, assertive businessman's voice. "I'm quite an experienced judge of talent and believe me you have the talent."

"Thank you. Can I, may I think about it overnight?"

"Of course, Simone. Here's a little bonus money up front to show you how serious I am about this," I said, while I watched her flush with ill-concealed excitement as I handed her two hundred dollar bills.

"Yours to keep," I said. "No matter what you decide to do."

"Oh, I couldn't," she said, making hand contact with me for the first time as she tried to give it back.

"No, no, you have to take it or I'll feel hurt and very disappointed," I said, turning my hands into fists so I couldn't take the money. I thought then, though perhaps I imagined it, that her eyes were tearing up as she finally took it.

"You think it over and when I meet you tomorrow after work you can let me know what you decide."

Another close to sleepless night. I couldn't stop picturing what it might look like. First I'd picture what I'd have to do to get to see it, the words I'd have to say, the money that would change hands, the alcohol we'd have to drink. Then I'd start picturing what I'd finally get to see. There were many different pictures too because it was a great mystery. In one I'd imagine it still there the size of a normal man's, or even a well-endowed man's, only with the pubic hair shaved the way she shaved her arms. In another I pictured it taped behind her like a kind of tail.

In others, it was a little stub not quite sculpted into a vagina, in others still she already had the beginnings of a clitoris. In the next wave of pictures I began touching it, no matter what she had or didn't have there—that's when I went to the kitchen, turned on the stove and forced myself to stare at the flame.

There is nothing stronger or more perfect than a flame. Fire started the world and fire in the form we call the sun will end it. Fire rules us, has absolute power over our life and death. The sun may not be God, but it's certainly one of God's most powerful agents. A flame is but an image of God, but that's enough to met out human justice on this earth. I reminded myself of all this as I held my finger less than an inch from it until the pictures of Simone slowly, slowly burned away.

You have a dream but you don't know what to do with it, not wanting to look either behind or ahead of yourself. My dream came in the morning just before the sun woke me up. I was skating with my older brother on a frozen pond, trying to catch up with him and must have put too much pressure on the ice. I felt the cold water under the ice rising up over my eyes just before I woke up.

I thought I'd left enough materials on my office desk for it to look convincing. I'd gotten some boxes and a few other things from Office Depot the day before. There were also a fairly large number of books in my home so I told her it was a book marketing business—not that she seemed very curious about it. In her car I sat a more than polite distance away from her. I was pleased that her conversation was reasonably relaxed.

"Thank you again for the opportunity," she said, and I said, "Thank you."

I live in a wealthy suburb where the poorest inhabitants would be upper middle class almost anywhere else. Judging by her wide-eyed response I thought this wasn't lost on her. At last my money is paying off, I thought to myself. It allowed me to control my aggression and project a relaxed, confident manner—qualities that women always find appealing. Despite waiting so long for this, despite thinking about it so much and so intensely, I was acting triumphantly low key. I thought now that I would suggest we have a bite to eat before getting down to business. Thought we could go somewhere unostentatiously classy like The Wine Bar, although I had a fear of sorts that the maitre'd or waiter would address us as "you guys." I suddenly wondered why Simone didn't wear lipstick or any makeup for that matter! I wondered why her hair was so short (although it was getting a little longer). Why not do one overtly feminine thing to help the general public? Did she secretly revel in confusing them?

We're having our first fight, I thought to myself, though oblivious to my thoughts, Simone was just then commenting on how lovely the weather had been lately—a warm November after the coolest summer anyone in St. Louis could remember.

In The Wine Bar, Simone had two glasses of wine to accompany her veal scaloppini and began to transform with very little coaxing from me.

"I've never done the kind of work I'm going to be doing for you, and I guess it's making me a little nervous," she confessed before she downed her second drink.

You've never been a woman either, I thought,

compared to which my job must be pretty small potatoes as far as new experiences go. I didn't say that, of course. What I said was, "That's why I brought you to The Wine Bar to get you relaxed a little. But I'm not nervous about you. I know you can do the job. How does that wine taste by the way?"

"It's very good."

"I think I'll have some too if that's all right with you?"

"Of course, Phil," she said, as I turned and looked for my waitress. It didn't take long before she materialized.

Later, Simone said, "Oh no, I couldn't," covering her mouth suddenly with her hand as if it were a sin to even dignify my question of whether she'd like a third drink, with any kind of considered answer.

"Oh, sure you could," I said. "You work very hard at the UPS store five days a week."

"Sometimes six."

"Really?" I said in a shocked voice, although I'd memorized her schedule a long time ago.

"Oh yes, every other Saturday I work there, too."

"Well, that doesn't sound right. You deserve to live a little."

"Am I doing all right?" she asked, her innocent gray-blue eyes locking onto me.

"You're doing fine," I said, as I once more signaled to the waitress. So far, my making the decisions was working out pretty well, I thought, as I felt some definite stirrings inside me, something that only happened to me lately when I thought about Simone.

When we got to my place Simone was definitely a little tipsy and so was I.

"Your place is so big and beautiful, and I

love all the candles," she said, pointing to them as if she'd just spotted a rare animal at the zoo. My living room was entirely lit by candles. As I suspected, the orange light was quite flattering for Simone, who was wearing a bright yellow shirt and her inevitable jeans.

"Thank you, Simone. Why don't you sit down on the sofa and relax for a minute?" I said earnestly enough.

She looked at me with a slightly confused expression before sitting down a little awkwardly but still in an unassumingly charming way. I quickly sat beside her.

"So, how are things in your life these days?"

My question appeared to have surprised her even more.

"Oh, things are fine, I guess."

"Things going along smoothly then?"

"Yes, mostly."

"No changes of any note?"

"Well this new job you hired me for is a change. Can you tell me what I'd be doing a bit more?"

"Of course I can, and I will. I just thought we could talk for a few minutes more and get to know each other a little. I think people work best when they get to know each other first and can be more open with each other, don't you?"

"I suppose so," she said in an uncertain voice, echoed by her uncertain eyes.

"Don't you think employer and employee should be absolutely honest with each other?"

"Yes."

"I mean not just in professional matters but in every aspect of their lives?"

"But wouldn't their relationship just be a professional one?"

"Oh no, not at all. I guess that's where I have a philosophical difference with you. I believe much more in the Japanese system of running a business, where they treat each other like family. And just as there shouldn't be secrets in a happy family, there shouldn't be any between employer and worker."

Simone looked both confused and temporarily discouraged.

"Do you have any secrets from your family?" I asked her quickly in as normal sounding a voice as I could manage considering I was almost trembling with excitement.

Immediately she looked away from me.

"Some."

"Some what?" I asked, wanting to hear her say the word.

"Some secrets."

"And what are those secrets about?"

She looked down at the floor.

"I don't feel comfortable talking about it."

"Now, see, that's just what I'm talking about," I said, getting up from the couch as if I'd had a revelation. I got up, but I didn't go far. I had my best bottle of wine already opened before I met her at the store. Beside the bottle were two wine glasses on a small, circular glass table by the sofa.

"You definitely need another glass of wine. I've brought out my best."

"Oh, no, Phil, I couldn't."

"But I've already opened it so you can't say no."

"Really, I shouldn't," she said while I was already pouring for each of us.

"But why in heaven's name not?"

"It will disrupt my thinking. Don't you want me to think clearly?"

"I want you to be honest," I said, handing her a drink. She thanked me for it, in spite of herself. I reached out and gently pushed back a few strands of her hair that were loose on her forehead. Her hair felt extraordinarily soft. After I did that her cheeks reddened.

"I just feel confused about what you mean and what..."

"Drink," I said authoritatively. "Drink it now."

She took a swallow. "Couldn't we start talking about the project now?"

I ignored her remark and, reaching into the pocket of my sports jacket, removed my wallet. "So Simone, did you enjoy the little gift I gave you yesterday?"

"I brought it back to give to you. It was very kind but..."

"What? Why would you do that? I told you that money was yours."

"In case you changed your mind. I mean, I didn't do anything to deserve it."

"My dear child, you do everything to deserve it. I want to give you a lot more, too," I said, removing ten hundred dollar bills and putting them on the table.

"But I haven't done anything yet, for the project."

"We'll get to that project. Right now the project I'm concerned with is Project Honesty, and since we're in a business relationship, I'm prepared to pay you for your honesty. It works like this: the more honest you are the more I'll pay you. That's right, now go on, finish the glass."

"I don't understand what you want me to be honest about," she said, setting the just finished glass down on the mahogany table near her where a candle was burning.

"The secret that you're hiding from your family and probably from a lot of other people, too. I want you to tell me that story. Believe me, I still have a lot of secrets I keep from my parents."

She looked away without saying anything.

"Is there anything else I could be honest about instead," she finally said.

I laughed. "Oh yes, indeed. As I said the more honest you are the more I'll pay you and you need money pretty badly don't you?"

"Yes."

"Because of your secret you really do need money. You see, I already think I know your secret, don't I?"

"It's not that much of a secret, at this point," she said.

"No, no it isn't. That's why I'm surprised you don't want to tell me about it. But I tell you what, if you show me your secret, I'll pay you twice as much. That's two thousand dollars just to show me."

"You don't mean that, do you, Phil?"

I realized then I shouldn't even tell her what option three was yet, for which I was willing to pay considerably more.

"Yes, I do mean it. That's how much honesty, your honesty, means to me. Look, I understand some people have trouble talking about things so that's why I'm also offering you, for twice the money, the chance to simply show me where you won't have to say a word."

"But that would mean I'd have to..."

"Yes, I know what it would mean, but it would just be for a few seconds. You think about it. You need money, and I'm offering you a lot. Not just today but if we work together I could pay for the whole thing."

"No, I couldn't," she said, making a gesture to get up and leave.

"Couldn't what? Show me, or let me pay for everything? Doesn't matter, the answer to either question is the same, yes you can. Just like the President says—yes you can. That's the answer."

I took another thousand dollars out of my

overstuffed wallet before she could move and placed the money where she could see it on the table.

"So, what do you say? Why are you hesitating? Do you have someone?"

"I did," Simone said, eyes on the floor again.

"Someone who was going to pay for things?"

"I thought I did."

"Well now you have me, who really cares about you, to help you. Someone you can count on a thousand percent."

"I just can't, really, I can't."

"Can't?" I said. "Before you give me an answer like that, I want to tell you a story from my life, okay? You could say I'm leading by example, if you want, by telling you the ultimate secret of my life. It won't take long so please, please listen."

I went on to tell her the story of my daughter. I had never had a daughter or any other child, but I didn't think she'd know I was lying. I'd told this story at other times in my life and been believed and even told it to myself so much that at times even I half believed it. It was a story about raising my daughter as a single parent after her mother left me. A story about extreme parental devotion to an emotionally troubled, but adorable, little girl. I described the toys I bought her, all the games we played and built. I described the daily stories I read her on end or made up. I described how I cooked and cleaned for her and changed all her diapers. Then I told her about the sixteen trips I took with her to places all over the world— London and Paris and Argentina and Madrid, California and Washington D.C. and Chicago and Boston and Florida. I mentioned how my devotion to my emotionally needy daughter cost me any chance of a relationship with a woman and was ultimately the reason why the great love of my life walked away from me. But I also described how my daughter's behavior improved, how her temper tantrums turned instead to laughter, how she slowly developed into a joyful, creative person who was finally able to feel and express empathy for others.

I saw how quickly and totally I got Simone's attention with my story and saw how each of the emotions she felt registered in unedited form on her soon-to-be woman's face. She had no problem feeling empathy. But now, it was time for my story's conclusion. This would be difficult. I had to describe how my daughter died, how she drowned in Costa Rica, the victim of a vicious, sudden rip-tide that took her out to sea and buried her in her beloved ocean. How had she escaped from my ever-vigilant eye? She had snuck out early in the morning while I was sleeping (we were staying in a resort that was right on the beach). It was her love of the sea that did it, that she couldn't resist so she changed into her bathing suit and tiptoed out of the room in the half-light of early morning, drawn by the little death flame of the rising sun before the lifeguard or anyone else was on the hotel beach.

"Of course I was crazed with grief after it happened," I said, "and considered suicide many times after she died. But then I decided to try to help others; that that's what my daughter would have wanted. That it was therefore the only way my life could make sense and be bearable."

"Oh my God," Simone said, finally placing her empty glass on the table, as if she'd been afraid to make a sound during my long monologue. I thought I saw tears sliding down her face.

"And now I've met you and want to help you. Do you see?"

"I'm just so sorry for you."

"Thank you," I said, still feeling close to tears myself.

"When did that happen to her, to you?"

"A little more than a year ago. The anniversary of her death was just before Halloween. She loved candlelight, too. That's why my home is full of candles."

She started crying softly again.

"Please," I said, "please stop crying. Could you just give me a hug?"

A moment later Simone was in my arms for the first time, though I thought it best to release her after a few seconds. But Simone was still silently crying and stayed in my arms of her own free will while I gently stroked her hair. Meanwhile, I had an unusual train of thought. It began with my wondering why I was so shaken by the story and why, when I told it, especially this time, did it almost seem true? Then I thought if I had had a daughter that is the type of thing that would have happened. If I'd had a child I would have lost it, the way I'd lost every person I'd ever loved, one way or another, to one degree or another. Or perhaps that wasn't it at all, and the story was about me and how I "lost" the closeness with my father I once had when I was very young symbolized by my "child's" drowning. I didn't know; I couldn't be sure.

Whatever the reason I'd told it again, Simone was still in my arms and I heard myself half whisper, "You can be my child, let me help you."

Only then did she disengage and look at me with an expression of both compassion and fear.

"How are you feeling?" I asked.

"My head is spinning."

"Lie down on the sofa," I said, suddenly getting up. "I'll go get you some Tylenol."

Simone didn't look in good shape when I returned to the sofa. "Here, swallow this," I said, lowering the glass to her lips. I waited for her to swallow, hovering over her in her yellow shirt and jeans, and then put the glass on the table by the sofa, a table now completely covered with hundred dollar bills. I suddenly knew what to do next. I gathered up the twenty hundred dollar bills in my hands.

"Sit up, Simone. In fact, stand up. You'll feel better."

She looked at me dizzily and almost passively and finally stood up, grasping one arm of the sofa to help steady herself.

"Here, this is yours," I said, stuffing the money into her jeans' pockets before she could protest or ever react. "Now you have twenty two hundred dollars towards helping you get what you want." I began unzipping her jeans.

"What are you doing?" she said weakly, as if it took all her strength to focus on what was happening to her.

"Simone, you have taken my money; you have taken my heart. Don't be so precious to yourself. It will just make me happy for a few seconds, just to look at you, not even to touch you. Come on, I thought you wanted to help me too?"

I'd now succeeded in unzipping her jeans and lowering them down her shaven legs. "But it's not ready," Simone protested. "It's not pretty yet."

I didn't say anything to that. I simply lowered her pants below her knees, then did the same to her delicately white panties until they were down as low and then looked at a tilting to the left, but otherwise normal-looking penis—normal except that all the public hair had been shaved.

Simone gasped then. It was almost a ghostly sound, horrified and restrained at the same time, as she turned away to dress herself. I had hoped for something different of course, from her and from what she showed me. Some surge of excitement instead of piercing regret and sorrow.

Simone sobbed for just a few seconds, then stopped and concentrated on getting dressed and out of my home as quickly as she could. When she was dressed and in possession of her pocketbook and car keys she headed for the door accompanied by me.

"Simone," I said, "I'm sorry if this hurt you."

"It's okay. You didn't make me do it."

"No, it's not okay. I want to pay for your operation, no strings attached."

"I don't want anymore of your money, ever. I wish you wouldn't come to the store again either, except when you know I'm not there."

"Only if you'll promise to keep working there, and you'll see, good things will happen. I will help you yet," I said, half to myself, as she shut the door and disappeared into her car and then into the night.

You are outside in the dark but inside you have a house full of candles—a maze of flickering, but constant, light. With light it isn't clear that you'd even need a god, you could always just look ahead. But fire is different. Its flame reminds you of what you can't forget.

I walked through the maze of firelight to the glass table where my money had once been by the sofa and where Simone had once been and in a sense would always be. Without hesitation, I put my thumb and index finger into the flame. It was pure and strong like our father the sun and gave me the pain I deserved.

THE MEMORY CENTER

There was a framed sign that hung on Dr. Rohr's office wall, even before Memo became widely discredited. No doubt it was an attempt to add a little humor to what otherwise was dominated by the typical procession of doctor's degrees and honors. The sign said, "If you forget everything you're an animal, if you remember everything you're a monster." The sign always made a deep impression on Foster, and during the time when both Memo, which exponentially increased people's memory, and Oblivion, that achieved the nearly opposite effect, simultaneously lost so much credibility (Oblivion finally even becoming illegal) the sign, which turned out to have been written by Dr. Rohr, himself, seemed to Foster nothing less than prophetic.

How proud he was in those days, often called the downfall of memory aids or Doma, to be a patient of Dr. Rohr's. How wise and steadfast like a great rock among water-driven pebbles the doctor was for never giving in and prescribing either drug to him—despite his passionate entreaties. Somehow Rohr himself knew better. "There's been a rush to judgment about both of these drugs—neither has been adequately researched, so I consider both Memo and Oblivion highly dangerous."

"Why are so many people claiming it's saved their lives, then?" Foster had once asked Dr. Rohr.

"People will say anything for money, Greg, the pharmacological industry more than most. Don't you see, they discovered that memory products sell," Dr Rohr said, with his characteristically raised eyebrows (that called attention to his slate-grey, unwavering eyes). "So Memo and Oblivion became part of the culture. You make money— you become culturally significant. But we don't have to be part of that culture, do we?"

Dr. Rohr could be electric, Foster thought. The fact that Rohr had summoned him to his office today not for a regular appointment but to discuss "something significant" excited Foster and all but completely filled his thoughts. He tried to distract himself, to little avail, by looking at some of the video art on the waiting room walls. He hadn't been so stimulated since he was a child and his father would call him into his in-house office on occasion to announce a trip to the beach or perhaps just to say he had tickets to a ballgame. His father had once been electric, too.

Over the years Foster had, unconsciously at first, studied Dr. Rohr's face with its subtle but surprisingly wide range of expressions. The moment he sat down in Rohr's office and looked at him, he knew the discussion would be important on a level that nothing they'd talked about over the years had ever been.

"Thank you for waiting, Greg. Now please come in," Dr. Rohr said in his earnest but slightly removed way.

Foster felt completely tongue-tied and merely nodded.

"It's wonderful to see you, and I'd love to catch up, but I'm a bit pressed for time so would you mind if I get right to the point?"

"Of course not, Dr. Rohr."

"We've had a number of discussions, in the past, some of them quite animated, about your depression, which I believe is far more serious than you realized and was caused by certain specific traumatic memories. We also discussed the possibility of your being helped by memory replacement therapy—a program you've expressed a great enthusiasm for. Is that still the case?" Dr. Rohr said, eyebrows taking flight again.

"Yes, definitely," Foster said, painfully aware that he had yet to speak a sentence longer than four words.

"Wonderful. I say that because research has now progressed to the point where we can finally, safely, begin a memory replacement program with you."

"Really?" Foster said, feeling his heart beating.

"Really."

"But, remember, this will take a special courage, not because we think the program is dangerous, because we don't, the risk factor is extremely minimal, but because the program is newer and as far as the lay public is concerned, it's still essentially untested. So you would be, in essence, a kind of pioneer. Are you feeling brave these days, Greg? Are you feeling like a pioneer?"

"Yes, doctor, I think so."

Dr. Rohr leaned in toward him in his navy

blue sports jacket, like an approaching wave in the ocean.

"I'm being extremely candid with you, Greg, tremendously candid. I'm telling you about the risk factor, for example, though I personally don't think there is any because, well the ethics of the situation requires it, first of all, and because I wanted you to ask yourself if you really are a pioneer. Well, Greg, are you? Ask yourself and then tell me before we take another step forward on this journey."

Dr. Rohr was leaning forward slightly in his chair now, and Foster knew what he had to say.

"Yes, Dr. Rohr. I definitely am ready."

"I have looked inside your 'yeses' before, and I have looked inside your 'nose'. And, God knows we have spent many hours inside your 'maybes,' and so, Greg Foster, I believe you."

"Thank you, Dr. Rohr," Foster said, smiling for the first time.

"I believe you and I believe in you. Now are you ready to hear the details of your mission?"

The word "mission" made Greg inhale a bit more deeply, but he knew Dr. Rohr was fond of military metaphors and had even confided in him once his frustration that the Iraq war had ended before he was old enough to participate.

"We want to begin a memory replacement therapy program with you at once. Is that exciting enough for you?"

"Yes, Dr. Rohr, but can I ask how long the program will take?"

"Two-and-a-half, three weeks tops. You're worried about your job aren't you? You still have an out-of-home office, is that it?"

"Partially out of home. There's a committee room I have to report to a couple times a week in person."

"In person?" Dr. Rohr said.

"My boss is pretty old fashioned."

"Well, the good news is most of the therapy is out-patient. We'll only need you for observation and testing in The Memory Center for the first few days so I don't see any obstacles there, do you?"

"No, I don't see them either."

"Which means they probably don't exist. Now it goes without saying that what I've told you and what I'm about to tell you is highly confidential and absolutely top secret. In fact, to follow protocol, I'll need you to sign various legal and medical forms now before I can fill you in on the details. But that shouldn't be a problem, should it? First we sign and then we talk, okay?"

"Of course, Dr. Rohr."

As if his meeting with Dr. Rohr weren't momentous enough, Foster had to stop taking Memo cold turkey, (he confessed to a disappointed Dr. Rohr that he'd been getting Memo on the street for almost seven years) and without the help of a real bridge drug, merely a tranquilizer he'd never liked called Equanimity, he found the transition difficult.

"When you stop taking Memo you may experience a slight headache or dizziness within the first 24 hours," Dr. Rohr had said. "You may also have intermittent feelings of anxiety. After all, your powers of perception and retention are returning to their pre-Memo state, and it will take a little while for your brain to adjust to its sudden, enormous loss of data. To avoid exacerbating this—and it will only increase your anxiety and feelings of impotence if you don't—try not to remember any particular part of your life. If memories come naturally of their own accord, fine, so much the better, but try not to increase them. The results might be too frustrating.

Meanwhile, you can do your work, even visit your office, though extended conversations will be difficult and should probably be avoided. In a word, try to live in the present as much as possible while your brain adjusts to its new loss of memories. You may feel sad at the paucity of your pre-Memo memory but be reassured that new powers of memory are on their way and that you'll never have to experience your most painful memories again! Think of that, my lucky pioneer. You're going to step into a new world, a new life, in a very short time. You'll still be you, but those memories that tormented you for years will be weeded out and eliminated. How about that, does it sound like it will be worth a little unpleasantness while you detoxify from Memo? By the way, as a medical precaution, we'll be sending you to our Memory Center after a week where we can observe you and the other pioneers more closely. We'll do it on a weekend so you won't be missed at work. Don't look so concerned. You'll find that being in the company of others going through the same experience as you can be quite reassuring."

"But I thought I was the only one doing it." Foster said. Of all the disconcerting things Dr. Rohr had said (which he later realized were, in typical medical fashion, understated) the fact that others would be included—not just him—was somehow the most disturbing.

"For the experiment to gain credibility, we need a statistically relevant sample. Don't worry," Rohr added, with one of his thin-lipped smiles, "They'll be enough glory for all of you later. Believe me, I know glory is a great motivator."

A feeling of weakness and a persistent desire to return to sleep overwhelmed him his first morning in The Memory Center. Yet he couldn't go back to sleep as if some part of his recently altered brain was preventing it, demanding instead that he deal with the weakness, fuzziness, and sometimes utter blankness that he felt when he tried to remember anything. "It's adjusting," he said, repeating Dr. Rohr's phrase from the last session. "Give it time, it's adjusting."

At least he had a private room, though there was too much white in it (as if it he were living in the snow). There wasn't even a single green plant to relieve the intense whiteness of the room nor were there any paintings. Then he remembered that Dr. Rohr had told him not to "panic in the white room." That it was part of the recovery process while he detoxified from Memo, that he have as little visual stimulation as possible the first 24 to 48 hours.

Maybe everything is going as it should, Foster thought, and I just have to be patient—always a problem for him, he realized. After all, hadn't he just remembered Dr. Rohr's warning about "the white room effect"? That proved his memory was still functioning, didn't it?

The next day he was supposed to have an optional monitored visit to one of his neighbors— the memory transplant patient who was both attractive and seemed to be staring at him at group counseling last night. He was never an especially aggressive person, but this time he decided to take the initiative. He really couldn't stand to be alone anymore.

He looked for his cpad (communication pad) so he could forewarn her about his visit but for some reason, he dimly recalled, it had been confiscated. He would have to take his chances and visit the old fashioned way by knocking on her door. He knocked and waited, still feeling so light-headed that he didn't think he could remain standing more than a few seconds.

"Who is it?" a woman's voice said.

"It's your neighbor, Greg Foster. Just came over to see if you might want to talk. You know, our monitored visit."

"Is that on the schedule?"

"Yes," Foster said, thinking how could you not know what's on the schedule? Could she possible have lost it? What if he, Foster, had lost the schedule? He would die of shame in front of Dr. Rohr.

"Well, come in, I guess."

Her room was like his in area and lack of design but the light in it was softer and more yellowish than white.

He told her his name again, and she said hers was Nadine but made no effort to shake his hand. "You can sit on that chair," she said, pointing to a grey upholstered, old-fashioned, straight-back chair about six feet from the one she was sitting in.

For a half minute they were silent and Foster thought of Dr. Rohr's saying, "Silence is just another noise we haven't heard yet."

"So," Nadine said, gesturing glibly with her left hand, "You having any second thoughts about the mission?" She said, the last two words with unmistakable sarcasm.

"What mission are you talking about?" he asked, although, of course, he knew.

"The one where they murder our memories and so murder us," she said, looking hard at him with her intense, cat-like eyes. In contrast, her hair looked listlessly yellow, like a faded photograph of itself.

"Why do you look so shocked?"

"Do I?" Foster said, still trying to regain his composure.

"Yeah, you look like you've just been electrocuted, actually. So, what is it? Speak up while you still can."

"It's just the words you used surprised me."

"I bet it's also surprising to have your old, pre-Memo memory back, isn't it? Feels a little empty, doesn't it? But think how empty it will feel when that goes, too, to be replaced by what? A chemically constructed new set of "happy" memories? Or maybe it will be more like a blank slate that gives you a second chance at being a person, if that term still applies."

"You seem very upset about The Memory Center. Very upset and very distrustful."

She laughed bitterly. It reminded him of the way his father laughed when he told him as an adolescent that he wanted to be a wall concept artist. Ironically, that was now as oddly a pleasing memory as any memory of his past life was.

"God, look at you. You're perfect. I can see why they picked you for the experiment," she said.

"But they picked you, too, didn't they?" he said curtly. "If you feel so negative about it, why are you here?"

She smiled in a tight, pinched way as if her bitterness had been transferred from her speech to her lips themselves. She had her hands on the sides of her formless, beige sack dress that hid what Foster suspected was a very appealing body.

"You assume I'm here willingly?"

"Of course, I assume that."

"Well I'm not. And I'm not an ex-Memo addict either."

"What are you then?" he said, aware that his question was rude and already preparing a kind of apology.

"As far as memory drugs go, if I took anything it was Oblivion and that was just cool with me. 'Cept I got caught, and I was told I could either go to prison or do this so-called experiment. So, yeah, right about now, since I'm already in jail," she said, indicating her little room, "I'm thinking I made the wrong decision."

Foster looked at her closely. He'd had some

of the same thoughts in his weaker moments himself though he'd never told them to Dr. Rohr or to anyone else. Yet it also seemed impossible that what she'd said could be completely true. And could Dr. Rohr know about it? That would be as preposterous, as if the laws of gravity suddenly no longer applied.

Meanwhile she was studying his face again as if looking for traces of inauthenticity in a counterfeit painting.

"Why did you really come here?" she said at last.

"What do you mean? Why did you let me in?"

"I guess I hoped you'd see things the way I do about the experiment."

"In the hopes of what?"

"Okay. 'Cause I'm looking for help in getting out of here, alright? I'm not a believer like you. I guess they didn't consider me risky or important enough to brainwash like they did you."

"I haven't been brainwashed."

"Really?"

"And I'm sure if you speak to any of the doctors you'll be free to go."

She looked at him incredulously. "You're either a masterful actor they sent in to evaluate me or you're the most naïve person on the planet."

"Why do you exaggerate so much?"

"Why are you so blind to the obvious? Are you on some kind of denial medication?"

"I'm not blind," Foster said, looking at his watch as if to prove to her and himself that he could still see and, in part, to be sure he was following the schedule. He had eleven minutes left.

"I don't think you have a clue how things work here, do you?"

"I know what I need to know," he said, repeating a saying he'd heard repeatedly from his father. But in this case, was it really true? They stared at each other in silence.

"Really," she finally said.

He nodded, sneaking a look at his watch again. He had nine minutes now but how was that possible? Two minutes, of course, was not a long time but it didn't pass that quickly.

Meanwhile, Nadine had stood up and assumed a kind of prosecutorial position while she spoke to him.

"Have you met the Administrator? Do you even know who he is?"

"I work with Dr. Rohr. Is that who you're calling 'The Administrator'?"

"So you think Dr. Rohr is the man in charge? They really have kept you in the dark. There's a whole hierarchy behind this 'mission' as you call it. Dr. Rohr's just in middle management. He's really not much more than an old timey drug dealer. I guess he didn't want to tell you that and break your bubble since you seem to idolize him. I'm sure he enjoys the adulation."

"That's extremely insulting to Dr. Rohr. He's been my physician since I was a child."

"So that explains how you got into this."

"I got into it by my own free will. It was my decision."

"Really? But I'm sure your Dr. Rohr was influencing you with some tried and tested propaganda the whole time, not to mention feeding you a lot of 'medications.' You're starting to remember that now, you're starting to remember again, aren't you?"

"No, not at all," he said, shaking his head. But he was remembering, quite vividly, in fact, that Dr. Rohr had given him three new pills with instructions to double the amount he took each day. When he'd asked him why the increasing amount and what each pill was for, Dr. Rohr had waved his hand dismissively as if his questions were both trivial and inappropriate. "Trust us, Greg, we know what we're doing." Foster had immediately dropped the subject but couldn't help feeling a residual unease about it.

"Well you're deep in thought about something," Nadine said. "If you ever do start to see things differently you can visit again though there isn't a hell of a lot of time left to get out of here. I hear they're going to start the transplants and a whole new medication program tomorrow."

"How do you know all this?"

"You don't expect me to tell you that, do you? Especially since you're still on the other side."

"Why do you find it necessary to think in terms of sides. The doctors are on our side—don't you see that?"

She shook her head slowly. "Look, Foster, this isn't about the doctors and us—it's much bigger than that. You do realize there's a drug war going on all over the country, all over the world, actually. Five years ago, it was all about Memo and Oblivion, now the memory transplant people are moving in. You don't think the doctors are neutral do you? They're leading the war. Billions of dollars are at stake, don't you see? These people want to control the world."

Their eyes met and Foster turned away. He'd heard this talk before on the Supernet, even seen it on posters on the street.

"Well, you're certainly given me lots to think about."

"But not to talk about, right? I took a terrible chance telling you this. You can't say a word about it. You promise on your life?"

"Yes," Foster said, "I promise."

*   *   *

It happened a few seconds after he closed her door. A half-stifled scream, then a muffled moan. He looked up and saw two uniformed guards covering what was probably a man. The struggling body was only visible for a few moments before the guards covered it like waves over a slice of sand. Then a door was opened and shut and the blur of the three bodies disappeared into the room.

His first impulse was to follow them. He knew his father thought of him as essentially a coward and had called him that more than once. His father was right then, too. As a child, even as an adolescent and beyond, the world scared him more than anything else, from the spiders in his cellar, to the dark of night itself. Women, of course, were frightening, too. For a man now approaching his late twenties in the post-AIDS era often referred to as the Sexual Renaissance, he'd had relatively little sex with them. Certain types of men still scared him as well, but he'd learned how to avoid tension with them and had never gotten into a physical fight. So it wasn't surprising that his second, more lasting impulse, was to do nothing now about the man the guards took away. Maybe he would tell Dr. Rohr about it later. After all, he still trusted Dr. Rohr more than he'd once trusted his unpredictable father or his weak-willed mother, for that matter, who'd also died seven years ago. Nadine had tried to make him doubt, not only Dr. Rohr, but the whole mission. Clearly she was troubled and had her own agenda. He should have defended himself more vigorously when she was clearly insulting him and worse, Dr. Rohr, and yet he couldn't honestly say he regretted the time he'd spent with her.

He looked around himself, saw and heard nothing unusual, then finally returned to his room still three minutes ahead of schedule and lay down on his bed. When was the last time he'd talked at such length to a woman so attractive? Probably sometime in his freshman or sophomore year in college. He remembered that it happened two or three times in the school cafeteria, where, granted, other people were seated, talking as well, but then there was his "secret memory," secret in that he not only never told it to anyone but also only allowed himself to remember it on special occasions—as if the less he remembered it the longer and more powerfully it would survive. Her name was Claudia, who had shoulder-length blonde hair and was in his biology class. He'd been fascinated with her from the moment he'd bumped into her coming out of the main college library one day and had the presence of mind to quickly say hello and invent a question about the homework they'd been assigned. Never before had his mind worked so rapidly and effectively. Questions were followed by her sweetly cooperative answers, were followed by his oddly appreciative comments (odd because that was so rare for him) and so on for three, perhaps five, minutes.

Two days later, he saw that she had a boyfriend from their biology class. Foster was crushed. He'd even dared to dream that he could be her boyfriend and then he had to let the dream go. But the beauty of his memory was that if he protected it, he would always have it to call upon, that five-minute conversation near the steps of the library, when, despite the people passing by, they were magnificently alone, and he was as close as he'd ever been to falling in love.

He got up in bed with a start. Would he still have access to this memory after memory transplant therapy? And what about Nadine? Though he'd felt so many conflicting emotions, including anger, he'd also felt attracted to her. Would that memory, and the woman who caused it, also disappear? And what of that struggling body he'd seen being hustled away? He suddenly wanted to see Nadine again with an urgency that amazed him and yet there was no time today—the schedule forbade it. But how could that be?

He double-checked the schedule. Mr. Harvey, a medical assistant, would be giving him his daily physical exam in a matter of minutes. Assuming he passed that, he had another orientation lecture to attend by Mr. Oswald, or was it Dr. Oswald? It was hard to remember who was a doctor and who wasn't at The Memory Center. At any rate, Oswald was a kind of motivational speaker, and allowing for group questions, the meeting would take about an hour. He thought they'd break after that, before dinner, but when he checked again he realized he was scheduled for another private counseling session with Dr. Rohr. Moreover, there would be no dinner scheduled for him because tomorrow morning was his operation, and he was only allowed to drink water for sixteen hours before it. His last solid food would be eaten under the vigilant eye of Dr. Rohr who would be operating on him tomorrow morning!

Why had he spent all his time with Nadine stupidly defending an operation that secretly scared him and that he had many unspoken doubts about? And to think, she wanted to join forces with him, to escape The Memory Center together! But that was too painful to think of now. He had to force himself to be practical, while he still was himself and his memory had not yet been wiped clean like an incorrect answer on an old blackboard. Any moment Mr. Harvey would be knocking on his door to give him yet another physical. His best hope would be to see Nadine at the final orientation meeting where he had to find a way to sit next to her so they could, at least, in some manner, have the chance to communicate. He wasn't sure what to think of the transplant, but his father had always told him to only have surgery as a last resort, and he needed more information, more time. He knew that. He was breathing hard, perhaps hyperventilating, and lay down to get his breath back. Had his life really been too painful to recall? Did it demand to be forgotten via the operation or was the real reason he was doing it somehow connected to Dr. Rohr? This was difficult to think about, too, like some problem involving both metaphysics and calculus. Somehow it also involved his parents' deaths and his disappointing career as a commercial illustrator—in other words, his whole life or his memory of it.

When the knocking came he barely heard it but moved towards the door robotically and opened it. It was Mr. Harvey, a smiling, blue-eyed man who shook his right hand (his left was carrying a medical bag).

"Hey Greg. How are you? Came to check you before the big day."

It was approximately halfway through the cursory exam that Foster wondered what would have happened if Dr. Rohr were the medical assistant and Harvey was the doctor trying to convince him to have a memory transplant. Would he still have decided to do it? Wouldn't he have perhaps taken a longer time before he consented, demanding more detailed answers, more statistical data, and consultations with additional physicians? He thought it would take him a long time to answer this question. Instead, the answer was quickly apparent even as Mr. Harvey was checking his heart rate. No, he wouldn't have gone through with it so fast.

He was doing it, ultimately, because of Dr. Rohr, and now, also because of Dr. Rohr, he had lost his great chance with Nadine.

. . . He passed his physical as he knew he would. He was scheduled to have the memory transplant tomorrow at 10 AM. Mr. Harvey left his room like a smiling ghost. Would he remember him a week from now? Or had the doctors programmed his future memory so he'd forget and thereby couldn't ever sue any of them?

He sank back in his bed and closed his eyes—his mind flooded with images of Nadine. Maybe he could will himself to sleep? Even if he missed the orientation meeting, would that be so bad? What would they do to him? What could they do to him if he stopped cooperating—cancel his operation? No, now that he'd passed his physical, he'd be given the procedure, no matter what. They needed him for their data. They needed him to complete their statistical samples. And if he protested they'd just give him a shot and knock him out. No one ever said he had to be awake to have the operation.

He kept his eyes closed and reviewed again not only the words but the visual details of his meeting with Nadine. He wondered if he'd be able to direct his thoughts like that again after the transplant. He got to his feet again, determined to go through with his original plan and talk to her at the meeting. In fact, there might be time to talk to her now, he thought, as he raced out of his room and began knocking on her door.

"Nadine, I need to talk to you. It's Greg Foster. Please, there's still time to talk. Let me in, please."

He listened, ear pressed to the door, the way Harvey had listened to his heart minutes before. Finally she answered from behind the closed door.

"What do you want?" she said, sounding a little breathless. Was she somehow having sex with someone in her room?

"I need to talk with you," he said.

The door opened. Immediately he looked beyond her but saw no one.

"What is it? What are you looking for?" she said.

"I wanted to see you about what we talked about."

"I'm too tired to argue with you anymore."

"You don't need to argue. I thought it over, and I think you may be right."

"So what does this mean? How did this happen?"

"It happened because I was finally honest with myself. You helped make me focus on things I was reluctant to face, things I'd been doubting for a long time. It means I'm ready to try to get out of here, if you still want my help."

Finally he dared to look at her and saw the faint trace of a smile.

"I might be the world's biggest fool trusting you, but beggars can't be choosers, can they?"

"I guess not," he said, offering a small smile of his own.

"I did Google you on the Supernet, just so you know I'm not a complete fool, and I liked your background."

"Didn't they take all your phones and computer?"

"I had a micropad computer. Don't bother looking for it. I hid it inside myself."

Foster blushed and looked away.

"Basically we have two choices. Attend the meeting and get out after it, or make a break for it now."

Foster tried to focus on the answer but saw only the shining white snow-light of his empty room.

"I think the meeting will be too well guarded," Nadine said, "I think our best chance is to leave now. And if you're working for the Memory Center, you can arrest me the moment I leave my door."

"Why would you think that? I'm just a patient like you."

"Ever notice there's a lot of lying in this world? Believe me, if it weren't for my micropad I wouldn't trust you no matter what. You should have gotten one and checked me out, too."

He thought of things left behind in his room—an old photograph of his father, a drawing he'd been working on of his father, too, made from memory.

"Can I get a few things in my room?"

"No, there's no time. Come on," she said, grabbing his arm as they went outside. He looked both ways as they left the building but saw no Memory Center personnel on the street, which looked filmy and lifeless as if it were old water in a dim aquarium.

"We have three minutes to get out of here," Nadine said, tugging at his hand again, as if he were a reluctant child.

"Where is everyone?" he said.

"That's what you'll be asking when you wake up from your operation, don't you think?"

Nadine was right, of course, blunt, maybe even a little more blunt than necessary, but that's what he needed now—the stark truth. Besides, when he thought about it, he realized that all the other overly obedient patients were already at the meeting in the Events Building.

They began running past a procession of grey buildings and tents that went on for three blocks, as if they were the center of a little city. At the end of it was a fence, though the guards, usually stationed there, were missing.

"Do we climb the fence?" he said. When he'd arrived at The Center he remembered with a shudder that he thought of the wooden fence as a charming, rustic touch.

"I think it's electrified."

"What do we do then?"

"We go through it anyway. The shock won't kill us. They want to examine us so they prefer that we live."

He wanted to object but followed her anyway, half shutting his eyes as if by doing that he could deny the electricity. Still, he hesitated for a second. It was odd. All his life he'd felt so much unnecessary nervousness but now it was really merited.

"Come on," she said, practically screaming at him. He closed his eyes and ran through it. He saw a pool of orange light, a flash of white, before he fell down.

When he woke up she was hissing at him like a snake. "Get up, Greg. There's no time."

"I've been electrocuted."

"You've been shocked. Come on, you can walk. I am."

She was moving in a zigzagging pattern but fast enough that he doubted he could catch up to her. He stumbled twice getting up, felt a sharp pain near his hip bone, but managed to lurch after her like a knight come to life on a chessboard.

They passed a group of skinny trees that he thought looked like old concentration camp trees. He wished he could examine them or draw them, but of course there was no time. Then he saw what looked like the skeleton of a town. Had it been bombed in the last war? He realized he was no longer sure what state they were in. He thought upstate Pennsylvania, but now he wasn't sure. He'd taken so many drugs they might have transported him and the other patients while they were passed out to one of the new states or to an unincorporated area.

Suddenly Nadine turned left with a purpose and appeared headed for a blank, three-story building that simply said "Hotel" in pale-blue letters. He'd thought of them as zigzagging knights for a long time, but now Nadine was walking in a straight line, and he had to imitate her in spite of his pain and dizziness, as best he could.

"Why are we going in?" he said, breathing fast and barely speaking above a whisper.

"I'm meeting a contact here. It's our only chance. Come on, hurry."

There was a tall but stooped man wearing wire rim glasses behind the counter. Was he the contact? At any rate, Nadine seemed visibly pleased and told Foster to follow her. He trailed slightly behind her, trying to look as inconsequential as possible until they reached the antique-looking elevator, still activated by buttons instead of by voice command.

"Why are we going to a room?" he said, knowing only that it was exactly what he wanted—to be alone in a room with her.

"Are you kidding? We'd be dead ducks if we stayed in the lobby."

"Is the contact meeting us in the room?" he asked, wondering if The Memory Center owned the hotel.

"Eventually."

"Was the desk clerk one of your contacts?"

"Hush. This elevator may have bugs on it."

"Really? It seems like it's on loan from a transportation museum."

She laughed briefly. It was the first time he'd ever seen her laugh. Maybe she was beginning to like him a little.

"Press open," she said.

The floor that billowed out before them was wooden and tilted slightly. It seemed to him the hotel could have been built in the 1980's and never been remodeled. How could it function, how could it do any business nearly 50 years later? He hadn't seen any other residents, and except for the desk clerk wearing those pathetically outdated glasses, hadn't seen any other people, either.

Meanwhile, Nadine was checking the door numbers.

"Here's our room," she said, stopping at number 33. She inserted the old-fashioned plastic key card and a small, under-furnished room appeared in front of them. He walked into the room, which at first seemed big to him only because it was a few feet larger than his room back at The Memory Center. He walked around several times, his leg now only hurting a little. The room had twentieth century style windows and bed. He looked at the window for a full half minute, saw a woman carrying a bag of groceries and a kid on an old-fashioned bike they'd stopped making 20 years ago.

"Is this a memory room?" he said.

"What do you mean?"

"One of those historical reenactment places that try to duplicate the past?"

"I don't think so. I think it's maybe some kind of holiday, like Founder's Day today and people are dressing up to look 1980s.

"But what about the way this hotel looks?"

"I wouldn't worry about it."

"Do you think it's owned by The Memory Center?"

"Why would you think that? Just because it's near the complex? They don't own everything, you know."

"They tried to own us," he said, thinking his acidic remark, which he still thought was an overstatement, might impress her. But she didn't seem to react to it.

"What, do you think, they're trying to bring us back to the past and stimulate our memory? They're trying to eradicate people's memories, not preserve them."

He nodded, though he was confused. How excitable, and quick to take offense, Nadine was! Maybe she was just nervous.

He sat down a polite distance apart from her on the bed, determined to change the subject.

"What do we do now?"

"The contact will be coming soon."

"To this room?"

"Yes," she said, simultaneously looking away from him and nodding.

They sat without talking for a few minutes or so until Nadine's voice bracelet rang. She spoke into the bracelet softly, in monosyllables.

"Yes. He's here . . . I see. It's blue, right?"

He tried to hear the voice on the other end but couldn't. A few seconds later she was off the phone.

"Our plans have changed," she announced.

"What happened?"

"Our contact got delayed. He won't be here for awhile."

"Was he going to get us transportation out of here?"

"He still will. He says it's better to lay low for now, anyway."

"And you completely trust this guy even though he's coming so late?"

"Yes, I do."

"And you think we should just stay here even though The Memory Center can break into the room any second?"

"They won't."

"How can you be so sure?"

"You ask a lot of questions, don't you?" she said, getting off the bed and then returning with her pocketbook. "Okay, look. I'm going to tell you something I probably shouldn't."

He looked at her closely. Was there no end to her secrets? And why was she still avoiding his eyes?

"I belong to an underground organization that opposes The Memory Center and everything it supposedly stands for. One of our main purposes is to save and deprogram people like you—victims who are slated for so-called memory transplants."

"You don't even think they're scientists at the Center, do you?"

"Do you? They're evil, maybe we should call them Evilists? That's all I can say about our organization except that we own this hotel so you're safe here. No transplanter would dare show up here, believe me."

"This is quite a stunning thing you're telling me."

"There's one other thing," she said, as she started rummaging through her purse. "I don't want to shock you, but we think these greedy, transplant frauds have already tried to screw with your memory."

"But that's impossible! My surgery isn't until tomorrow."

"That's what they told you. But they're already given you a lot of medication and therapy. I know about Harvey's visits to your room."

He felt his heart beat but told himself he shouldn't be so easily convinced. "So assuming that's true, what can I do now?"

"Fortunately, our scientists have been working on an antidote to the pills Harvey gave you. You need to take this," she said, her hand at last liberated from her pocketbook as she showed him a blue pill that could almost pass for the once popular sexual aid Viagra.

"It's called Identity, and it will give you back the memories they stole from you. Come on," she said, bringing the pill up to his face. "The sooner you take it the more effective it will be. Don't you want your own memories back in your mind where they belong? They really weren't so bad. It was Rohr who made you think they were."

He opened his mouth and placed the pill inside. But he kept his mouth clenched—the pill still on his tongue.

"Look, Foster, you have a kind of interesting mind, but we don't have time to discuss philosophical issues. You have to take the pill now and let it work. You just have to trust me."

"It's too bad they don't have a pill for that," he said.

"I'm sure it will happen but for now trust your identity pill and swallow it."

He saw the green in her eyes again and then closing his own, finally swallowed.

Within fifteen minutes he began to feel dizzy and asked if he could lie down. Nadine got up from the bed and sat in an antique-looking, straight-back chair in the corner. He struggled to keep his eyes on her as if to preserve the last beautiful image in the world. But when he closed his eyes, the pill took control.

. . . A door shut and he was inside a house like a fort in space. It was dark but there were hallways in front of him pulsating like tentacles, each one beckoning to him, urgently. He went down one of them and immediately realized he would never see the other hallways. But could he even remember what those had lead to? Suppose Dr. Rohr was in one of them or else his father?

How much of them could he really remember now? What was memory anyway? An image, a blur. On such flimsy, mentally manufactured material "reality" was constructed and society empowered. Memory is vanity and so is identity, he thought. They're both illusions.

"I can't remember anything," he said out loud, opening his eyes.

Nadine was beside him, sitting on the bed.

"Let the pill work. Identity will help you get it back."

He closed his eyes. Didn't she understand? His memory, like everyone else's, was almost totally deficient before the transplant. That's why Memo was such a popular street drug for a while, before it got legitimized.

He could feel the pill coursing through him, entering his veins like little rivers. The high was almost overwhelming, but he fought it so he could finish his line of thought. He remembered reading about America's psychedelic period in the 1960's and the comeback it had made a few years ago, nearly seventy years later. LSD gave people a sense of power with the pseudo wisdom it produced, Foster thought. But when people eventually saw through it, they tired of it and abandoned it again for drugs like Memo. But Memo led to suicides in some cases and incurable depression in others. Oblivion, a street drug that never made it to the FDA wasn't the answer either. By erasing as much memory as it could indiscriminately, Oblivion eventually created hundreds of zombie-like people, and while they rarely committed suicide, their public displays of apathy, addiction, and depression were appalling.

The Memory Center stepped into this void and claimed to have the answer by combining the best of the past drugs and synthesizing them into something new. " It purported to wipe previously powerful memories clean [which Oblivion did], create new and/or enhanced memories like Memo and finally, purportedly, give one increased wisdom or insight into the world like LSD did [although to his credit, Dr. Rohr always down-- played that aspect of it]. Yet, incredibly, he was abandoning Dr. Rohr now and putting his faith into a new memory aid.

"How are you doing?" Nadine said.

He nodded to signal that he was all right.

"I thought we were losing you for awhile." Nadine was smiling. She had unbuttoned her shirt as if to divert him by the partial sight of her breasts. But he couldn't be deterred.

"When you realize you're going to die still knowing nothing of the world, you see everything differently," he blurted. "Your life and everyone's is just an illusory little stage show. Some old people know this but we won't listen to them," Foster said.

"Do you know it?"

"I must know it now...By the way, you're very pretty," he said, staring at her breasts.

"I do what I can," she said, smiling in a charmingly crooked way.

"Sorry. I shouldn't be so direct."

"I've found that being direct is usually the best way to go. Excuse me," she said, reaching down beneath her underwear and removing a small blue object. "My micropad was starting to irritate me," she said, pointing to the phone.

He nodded. He was still very high.

"That's why I want to talk to you now while you're still completely coherent."

"Sure," he said, thinking he had never seen a woman do what she'd just done.

"I'm going to start by being very direct with you. Have you ever heard of the I.P.L?"

"The I.P.L? No."

"It stands for Identity Preservation League, and I'm a member of it."

"No, I haven't heard of it. What does it do?"

"Basically what its title says. We try to help preserve people's identity through promoting the use of the drug Identity that you just took and by holding seminars and sometimes interventions trying to prevent people from getting transplants. It's the organization I told you about before."

"Is that what you did with me?"

She looked away from him for a moment. "Yes, Foster, it is."

"But how did you know about me?"

"We know about Dr. Rohr. We know you were a patient of his. We have quite a lot of intelligence on Rohr."

"You hacked into his files?"

"It could be something like that. The important thing is we discovered you and what Rohr had you targeted for."

"He told me I was extremely depressed. I thought he was trying to help me."

"Of course you did. Dr. Rohr is a trained expert in identity manipulation. That's why we make monitoring him a top priority of our organization."

"But how did you get access to The Memory Center and then get a room next to mine?"

"Just because we're good people, you shouldn't underestimate us."

He stared at her. When he was seven or eight he remembered playing on a beach with a girl a little younger than him who wasn't wearing any top. It made him feel strangely at peace though also slightly titillated at the time. Now this reminded him that he still had his memory—and the erotic part of it, too. He felt flooded with gratitude, along with waves of attraction for Nadine in whom he now saw that little girl's face from his cherished afternoon at the beach. He wanted to tell her all this and much more, but he could only stare at her and her bare breasts she seemed to be holding for him.

"Identity is pretty incredible, isn't it?" she said.

He nodded or tried to. He was no longer sure of what he wanted to do and what he actually did. He was thinking very fast but wasn't sure yet if he had spoken at all. He was thinking that there are no geniuses really because no one understands the world. That even if Rohr's memory transplant worked, (which he now thought was highly unlikely) people still had to die and the mystery of the universe was still, and always would be, unsolvable.

"Do you think you'd like to join the Identity Preservation League?" Nadine said.

He was fairly sure he nodded this time.

"Good move, Foster. That's really good news," she said with an ecstatic smile. She went back to searching through her pocketbook. "I have the papers you'll need to sign right here or we could do it electronically by voice print."

Foster shrugged. Everyone these days belonged to an organization and often to two or more. He just hoped she didn't expect him to read it in the state he was in.

"I should tell you it's a lifetime commitment," she said, hands on her hips, breasts still exposed. Then he noticed that she was holding a pen as if it were a pet she was controlling with a leash until the papers reappeared like a little flock of birds.

"Come on, Foster. Sit up and sign these. You can move. Come on, try it and you'll see that you can. That's the boy, sit up a little more now. Come on, you're almost there. Climb that mountain, and I'll make you a happy man."

It was like climbing a mountain but knowing she was there at the mountain's top gave him the strength.

"Now sign, as clearly as you can for Mamma."

Somehow, though he could barely focus, barely move, he signed three times. She gave him a hug—so beautiful he was afraid to open his eyes. Then he sank back in his bed, hoping she was with him, and moments later fell asleep.

He'd been running for a long time—by an ocean whose waves were mounting. Finally he found shelter in a cave with Nadine but now she was shaking him violently.

He opened his eyes and she was still shaking him, but they were back in the hotel room, and she was completely dressed.

"Let's go, Foster. We've got to go. You've got to get up now."

"What happened?"

"You fell asleep. The plans have changed. We've got to get out of here and meet the contact somewhere else."

"But why?"

"There's no time to talk about this. Just get up from the bed now, okay?"

She looked scared. He still felt an afterglow from the high but stood up. It was easier than he thought.

"Good," she said. "Let's go."

"Can I use your bathroom? I have to pee."

"There's a bathroom in the hall but there's no time. Use the sink."

He felt his face redden.

"Come on, I won't look," she said, turning her back to him. He didn't think he could do it but he urinated in her sink. It felt a little like when he peed after smoking pot—only even more hot and sensual and longer lasting.

"You done? Let's go."

They went outside into the ostensible center of the town. Though they were hurrying, they couldn't really walk fast because their legs were still recovering from the electrified fence.

"Don't look at the town," she said, "especially not at any people. Just keep looking straight ahead."

There were precious few people to look at anyway and those few he did notice were all strangely dressed in some symbolic manner, he thought. One of them, with a long face and sharp blue eyes, did stare at him, but he quickly turned away though not without wondering if he were another patient gone AWOL like him.

He could understand Nadine not wanting him to make eye contact with any of the people who moved by them like shapes in a dream, but would it really be so wrong to look at some of the buildings? Whenever he thought that she wasn't noticing, he snuck a look at them. He was struck by how irrationally shaped they were, like prehistoric animals. One of them that they appeared to be headed towards looked like a slightly twisted dinosaur, and he immediately nicknamed it the Dinosaur Tower to himself.

"This is where we'll meet the contact," she said.

"It's a very weird looking building."

"You shouldn't be looking at it. I thought we agreed on that point."

"Sorry," he said.

"I'm serious," she said, with a sudden rush of anger. "Don't look at anything. Why doesn't anybody ever take me seriously," she muttered. Was she ignored by her organization as well? Was that why the contact didn't come to the hotel? He tried to follow her instructions but couldn't resist looking at an engraved sign above the door of the dinosaur tower. It said (unless he were mistaken) The Rohr Building—but how could that be possible? Did Rohr have a relative who worked for the other side?

Inside in the large, cavernous lobby a tall beautiful woman with long, straight black hair walked directly towards them accompanied by a man with a receding hairline and restless eyes. The woman wore a nametag with the word "Seven" on it. The man's nametag said "Wilhelm."

"Good afternoon," the woman said, extending her hand.

"Good afternoon," Foster said, shaking it.

"My name is Seven," she said, half forcing a smile. It was an unusual name but more and more people had been naming themselves after numbers, lately.

"I'm Greg Foster," he said, reluctant to let her hand go.

"Yes, I know. It's our job," she said, indicating the man beside her who was talking animatedly to Nadine, "to escort you to your destination."

Foster nodded. It was an odd way to put it—"destination," but Seven was otherwise being perfectly polite. Wilhelm, on the other hand, sounded almost cross as he spoke to Nadine, and Foster wondered briefly if he should intervene. But Seven beat him to it, tapping Wilhelm on the shoulder and then speaking rapidly in a foreign language that Foster thought was probably German. Wilhelm and Nadine continued with their own rapid-fire conversation, during which Foster tried to make eye contact with Nadine who was still looking straight ahead, soldier-like, as if reading a script.

Finally Wilhelm tapped him on the shoulder. Now it was time to shake hands again.

"I'm Wilhelm," he said in an accent, very similar to Seven's.

"I'm Greg."

"Good to meet you, man. Seven and I will be showing you the way upstairs," he said, eyes darting around as if a little loose in their sockets. "Are you ready to roll, man?"

"Ready to roll," he said, relieved that Nadine, though she still wasn't looking at him, had at least joined the group heading toward the elevator.

It was an old, slow-moving elevator, like the one in the hotel, one of the very few he'd seen since elevators became high speed twenty years ago. He found himself sneaking looks at Seven nearly the whole ride, in part because Nadine seemed so out of sorts, and was avoiding him, but also because of Seven's undeniable beauty.

When they got out of the elevator he and Nadine finally looked at each other. Her angry look was replaced by a strangely sad expression.

"Veel be splitting up now," Wilhelm said. "That's simply the vay we've been told to do it, man," Wilhelm said to him.

Foster nodded respectfully. Nadine said nothing—her expression still indecipherable.

"So then we go now. Don't look so glum, man. Help is on the way. It's my motto, you know. Maybe I should put it on my t-shirt to make it more real," he said with a little laugh. "So Lady N, you come with me," he said, taking Nadine by the hand. "Seven, meanwhile, will take care of you."

He was surprised that Wilhelm shook his head warmly as if saying goodbye at a party.

"Goodbye, Wilhelm. Goodbye, Nadine," he

couldn't help saying himself. She looked at him cryptically for a second before walking down the hall with Wilhelm. Meanwhile, Seven walked down a hallway in the opposite direction. He lagged a step behind so he could look at her body more easily and yet he still wanted Nadine. Why hadn't he made a move when her shirt was open and she was showing off her breasts? Why didn't he do something when he was high on Identity and alone in the room with her?

"Can you walk a little faster," Seven said. "We're running late."

"Sure," he said, as they turned yet another corner and a new giant hallway appeared in front of them. "It's like a labyrinth in here," he added.

"Maybe, but it's one you need to pass through."

"Who is it exactly that I'm going to see?"

"Didn't Nadine tell you?"

"She said it was someone from the Identity Preservation League."

Seven turned and looked at him for a moment. "That's enough for now," she said. "The rest you'll find out soon enough. Don't be too eager 'to learn.' That's people's problem in general."

What do you mean, he wanted to ask, but she had surged ahead of him, used her voice code, and with him still a half step behind, entered what looked to be a vacant waiting room with nature paintings strategically placed along the long white walls. It definitely had a Memory Center feel to it, Foster thought.

"Someone will be with you in one or two minutes," a robot behind a desk said. Seven looked nervous in spite of herself, which in turn increased his anxiety.

"Is this place completely robotized?" he said.

"No, some humans work here but it's not always easy to tell them apart."

He laughed but Seven didn't even crack a smile, and he quickly began to wonder if she meant it or not. Somehow the fact that she'd confused him again made him bolder, bold enough, at least, to return to his original question.

"What did you mean when you said being too eager to learn is people's problem in general?"

"My job is to escort you here not to explain my philosophy."

"Still the robot said we have a minute to wait. I was just curious."

He thought he saw a trace of emotion in her eyes. "No one is supposed to be interested in what I think, so why should you be?"

"Because it's an intriguing statement, and you're an intriguing person."

"Too bad you didn't get Wilhelm for your guide. He likes to elaborate on his view of the world but apparently he prefers working with Lady N, who after all, is renowned as a thinker," she said sarcastically.

"Is Wilhelm your husband?"

"No."

"Your boyfriend?"

She hesitated and he thought he saw her lips tremble. "You ask too many questions. But, okay, I'll answer one last time. Wilhelm is not my boyfriend."

"Really?" he said, feeling suddenly both indiscreet and jealous. "Is that really true?"

"He's my brother, alright, now stop asking questions. We wait now in silence, the way people always wait."

"I would love to see you again," he said, perhaps still being influenced by the Identity he took.

"See me or screw me?"

Her question froze him. Of course, the answer was both.

"You see how confused you are? Now let's wait in silence, okay? Don't make me signal for Wilhelm."

Foster tried to follow her advice, realizing very quickly that he needed to work on himself psychologically to calm down. Nadine and Seven were both confusing people or at least had already confused and frustrated him, and he knew he shouldn't appear confused when he finally met his contact, who might be a big-shot administrator at I.P.L. He blinked several times as if to usher in a new era of concentration. His freedom, the preservation of his mind—that was what really mattered. Ten seconds later the door opened, and walking ahead of Seven, as she directed, he entered an enormous, maze-like room.

Two men in dark suits and sunglasses (one seated at a desk) were at the far side of a room that seemed as long as a football field.

"Please come in," said a tall, pale-skinned man who was standing by the desk, gesturing with his preternaturally long, skinny arm. Trying to walk in a straight line, Foster crossed the room a few steps in front of Seven.

"I'm Dr. Rossi," the tall, almost gaunt man said, who resembled a scarecrow or an undernourished zombie. He extended his hand and Foster shook it, surprised at the strength of Dr. Rossi's grip.

"I'm Greg Foster."

"Yes, of course you are," Dr. Rossi said with a tight smile. "We know all about you," he said, picking up a notebook from the desk. "Well, not all about you but a fair bit," he said, pointing to the black notebook with his free hand. Were those his files?

"And this doctor I'm sure knows you even

better," he said, indicating the man at the desk who rose from his seat, took off his dark glasses and looked at him sternly.

"Hello, Greg. Yes, it's me, Dr. Rohr. I know you're surprised to see me. So I want you to sit down and let me explain some things to you. Does that seem fair to you?"

Too stunned to speak, Foster sat in a chair a few feet from Dr. Rohr.

"What does seem fair to you, I wonder? Do you think you've been fair to me? Do you think you were being fair when you told me you were ready to be a memory transplant pioneer and then violated my trust, the trust I placed in you, trust that I need to fuel my work, all destroyed as soon as a pretty girl said a few lies and sweet nothings to you?"

"Nadine?"

"That's the name you know her by. You tried to trick me and you failed, Greg. Moreover, in failing, you failed me and that I cannot tolerate."

"I'm sorry, Dr. Rohr."

Rohr put on his glasses again. "I shouldn't be shocked with all I've seen in this world. But I believed in you, and now that belief has turned to dust. People kept warning me about you, detecting a pattern of instability in you, a basic weakness especially when it comes to women. Finally, I concluded that I had to test you, and you sold me out within a day, that's how weak you are. That's how little you value my trust. And without trust in me the transplant won't work. That's the great irony of the situation. If you don't give me your total faith, it won't succeed; it won't and I won't. You look confused. What is there to be confused about? You behaved like an ape. You sold me out for a woman you didn't even know."

"But what about the Identity Prevention League?" Foster blurted, looking suddenly around the room before noticing an unmistakable smirk on Dr. Rossi's face.

"That only exits in your mind," Rohr said. "You were told it exists by N and you chose to believe her. Mind you, there are groups of malicious, destructive people who oppose the work I'm doing, and we are concerned about them. Great change always provokes great resistance. But they're too disorganized and basically stupid to have formed any organized resistance—much less a league. Much less the town you've just passed through. Those buildings are mine, Greg. Are you finally beginning to understand?"

Instinctively, he looked to Seven for help or at least sympathy, but she'd put on her own pair of dark glasses.

"I'm sorry I let you down, Dr. Rohr."

"Saying you're sorry is not enough at this point, not after all the time and trust I placed in you."

"What can I do to make it up to you?"

"That is the question, isn't it? First you'll need a complete reorientation program before your transplant. Seven will supervise. She's living proof that it can be done. Before she came to me, she and her brother Wilhelm were both addicted to Oblivion. I turned those addicts into transplant pioneers and in the process saved their lives. Isn't that true, Seven?"

"Yes, Dr. Rohr," she said.

"But what about my job?" Foster said.

"Once you're reoriented and have your transplant, you'll be working for us. My heart is a vast place, Greg. I've been hurt deeply by you, but I can forgive, too. I am the father of The Memory Center, Greg, the father of new memory. I am your father of fathers and you will place all your faith in me now, for I am truly your last and only chance."

*　　*　　*

Could a building be endless? How long had they been walking, he and Seven? There seemed to be windows everywhere but they were tiny, like the size of bats, so he was walking in a kind of perpetual twilight. There was one other time when he walked this long. He'd had a fight with his parents on the beach when he was about nine and had stormed off. When he got tired of being alone he couldn't find them at first. The distance back to them seemed infinite. So he still had that memory, at least for now. After the procedures, probably not anything of his parents, though Rohr assured him he'd have some "selective, peaceful ones." But he no longer believed in Rohr's reassurances.

Suddenly, Seven stopped walking and opened the door to a half-lit room about the size of the room in the hotel he'd been in with Nadine.

"Why isn't there more light?" he said.

"These are the best conditions for your transition."

"But, the whole building is like this."

Seven shrugged. "Sit down or, if you prefer, lie down," she said.

He was momentarily relieved that the room had a medical looking bed and cabinets but then thought again about his transplant.

"Is my operation going to take place here?" he said, still standing, in fact circling around his chair.

"I don't know. Why don't you try to relax a little. I'll sit and talk with you."

It was the kindest thing anyone had said to him in a long time, and he felt tears in his eyes as he sat down facing her.

"I'll be losing so many memories," he said. "It'll be like I'm losing infinity."

"We think you'll keep the necessary ones and be able to face life more purposefully," she said, stuttering on the last word, as if it were a foreign one she had only recently learned.

"Besides," she continued, "when your memories are cleared, it's like starting over and being free to experience a new kind of infinity."

"Is that what happened to you?"

She looked away from him.

"It's not important what happened to me."

"It is to me."

"You heard what Dr. Rohr said, I was an Oblivion addict."

"I don't know what that means."

"It means I took a lot of Oblivion."

"I mean I don't know what Oblivion does."

"You never took it?" she said skeptically, suddenly, also, staring at his face as if to verify his amazing confession.

"No, I took Memo for years but never Oblivion."

"Memo is the door to hell. Oblivion makes you forget hell, at least for four or five hours. It's kind of like a little memory transplant."

"So you had the transplant?"

"Of course. What kind of representative would I be if I hadn't?"

She looked away from him, and he sensed she was hiding something or perhaps simply lying.

"Wilhelm, too, has had a transplant. He's another living example of the transplant's success. We're both kind of like advertisements for it."

"Wilhelm? Your boyfriend?"

"I told you already he's my brother, didn't I?"

"You hesitated when I asked."

"Don't get hung up on my hesitations, alright? There are more important things, like can I trust you. Anyway, right now I need to use the bathroom. Will you be all right? I'll just be across the hall for a few minutes."

"Of course, I'll be fine."

She gave him a close look again. "I'll have to lock you in while I'm gone," she said before she turned decisively and left him alone in the room.

First, he tried the door, but she'd locked him in as she said she would. Then he noticed that she'd left her briefcase, which incredibly wasn't locked. In a small, zippered compartment he found two containers of Oblivion. So, she was still using and apparently under its spell enough that she risked being discovered as he himself just had. Then, he thought that perhaps she wanted him to know.

How long did it take a woman to urinate? Maybe there was more she had to do. He thought she could be back any second but continued looking through her briefcase anyway. There were a series of documents and ID cards and then an interesting letter he soon realized was from Wilhelm as well as one from Dr. Rohr, both signed "with love."

"What the hell are you doing?" Seven said, suddenly appearing before him as if she'd opened the door silently. "Nothing gives you the right to go through my things."

"Sorry, but I want to get out of here, don't you?"

"You have no right to search my things. I don't belong to you."

"It's a little late to worry about 'rights.' Nobody's looking out for mine. I have no Wilhelm in my life."

"I'll kill you if you say anything about him to

anybody. Maybe I'll kill you anyway." She said, taking a decisive step towards him.

"Dr. Rohr wouldn't like that either. Your job isn't to kill me, it's to deliver me so my brain gets gutted. Nadine did her job. You wouldn't want her to replace you, would you?"

"You're a pretty big talker considering you have no options."

"Don't be so sure. I know things that you don't."

"You're lying. You're gonna get your operation, just like I did, and you won't even remember this conversation ever took place."

"Is that what happened to you?"

"I just told you it did."

"Then why do you still take Oblivion?"

"I'll kill you if you tell anyone that. I really will."

"I'm going to have my mind killed anyway."

She looked away from him and paced for a few seconds.

"You want to have some kind of sex with me? Is that what this is all about?"

"That's very tempting, but it wouldn't really help my long-term problem, would it?"

"Don't worry so much about your operation. It's not that big a deal."

"You didn't have it, did you? For some reason you got out of it. Was it because of Dr. Rohr and what you did with him? Maybe that's what Nadine did, too."

"Shut up," she hissed, snake-like. "You don't know anything about it. Wilhelm and me were both abused in every way by our father back in Germany. We escaped together and lived all over the US. Dr. Rohr helped us. He rescued us. He's our new father. I don't agree with everything he does, but I owe him a lot, okay? He needs a lot of support, even more than what Wilhelm and me both give him every day."

"You mean he has a big appetite."

"Shut up!"

"Okay, so what do I have to do to not get a transplant? That's all I want to know."

She suddenly got calmer and for a few moments seemed to be seriously considering his request.

"There might be something I could say to Dr. Rohr to get you a trial postponement. I know he has a special interest in you, but you'd have to give yourself totally to him. And under no circumstances tell him about my Oblivion."

"What does 'give myself totally' mean?"

"Obviously you've never done it with anyone."

"I committed to Dr. Rohr in the beginning before Nadine talked me out of it."

Seven laughed cynically. "Are you sure all she did to change your mind was talk to you? I didn't think she was that smart."

"She's plenty smart."

"Sure, with her tits and pussy."

Foster paced off a semi-circle (fighting his desire for Seven) and said, louder than he thought he would, "I want to get out of here."

"I hear you. Look, here's the deal. You took some Identity today with Nadine, didn't you, but it's probably starting to wear off, right?"

He nodded.

"I have another half a tab for you. Okay? Sound good? I'd share some Oblivion but I could get in big trouble for that, and besides, I want you to remember what I told you about Dr. Rohr and how you have to accept him as your total father. Just think, after that you'll be my brother."

"Is that the way Wilhelm became your brother?"

"Wilhelm was always my brother. But Dr. Rohr made us even closer when he became our father. So here, take your medicine," she said with a little smile, "Best fucking medicine you'll ever take, right? Hey, I made a pun."

"What are we taking the pills for?"

"Don't you want to get high?" she said, looking shocked for a moment.

"But there's no time."

"There's plenty of time. I know how much time there is. I'm in charge of you, remember? We stay here until I get you ready for Dr. Rohr. So don't you want to have some fun with me— believe me you need it. I'm gonna take a little Memo later but for awhile I won't remember anything you do to me," she said, suddenly massaging his thighs and crotch. "Doesn't that sound appealing to you, big guy? Come on, we're wasting time," she said, as they both swallowed their pills. "Why don't we start by taking a nice, slow, oral bath."

It was like meeting in a chamber of the ocean. He emerged from underwater only to face the towering tidal wave of Dr. Rohr. Foster blinked, may even have shaken his head as if to goad himself into consciousness, but Dr. Rohr was still looming in front of him like a sea giant. Was there some pill or shot Rohr had taken that allowed him to gain a half-foot since he last saw him? There seemed to be a pill or procedure for everything else at The Center.

"As I told you, I was very disappointed to learn of your resistance to the therapy I offered." It was definitely Dr. Rohr speaking but the voice sounded as otherworldly as Poseidon's.

"Again, I'm sorry Dr. Rohr, please forgive me," he said, using almost the exact words Seven had told him to say.

"I spent a considerable amount of time researching you and getting to know you in general. I thought we had a special understanding, much like a father has toward his son."

"I'm sorry."

"To betray a father is the worst of sins, don't you think? And now you want to cancel your memory transplant that I'd been counting on. Did Seven put you up to this?"

"No, Dr. Rohr. I'm so sorry. I'll do anything if you'll forgive me and let me avoid the transplant."

Dr. Rohr smiled. It was like seeing a row of white caps on the sea.

"Do you want me to be your father again?"

"Yes, Dr. Rohr."

"Address me as your father then!"

"Yes, Father Rohr."

"I am told by my daughter Seven that you will do anything for me. Is that correct?"

"Yes, Father Rohr."

"Do you understand that if you disobey me again it will be a fate worse than death?"

"Yes, Father Rohr. It will never happen again."

"Do you understand and accept that I am also Wilhelm's father, and Nadine's, and everyone's father at The Memory Center?"

"Yes, Father Rohr."

"Do you understand that they worship me as a God."

"Yes, Father Rohr."

"Are you prepared to worship me in the same way and to prove your worship by doing whatever I say?"

"Yes, I worship you, Father Rohr."

Dr. Rohr unzipped his pants then as if he were emptying a useless pitcher of old water.

"Get on your knees and crawl towards me," Dr. Rohr said, pointing his shark-like penis at Foster.

Foster crawled towards him as if moving in warm, shallow water.

"Now, open your mouth as wide as you can; I've decided to let you keep your memory," Dr. Rohr said. "It will be filled with me."

Several months passed, or perhaps more than a year, since he'd been working on the farm in Rohr County. His simple, repetitive chores included sweeping the barn, disposing of the horse manure, fixing the more skilled workers breakfast and lunch, then washing the dishes, and cleaning the floors and toilet. People were often around him but rarely talked to him, either because they were too busy themselves, considering him of a lower caste, or perhaps were instructed by Father Rohr to shun him while he was still a novice, Foster couldn't tell. He thought of each of these theories as well as several others before he stopped thinking of them at all. Also, of course, he got used to what at first seemed an exotic sight of seeing so many people moving around him in almost geometrically precise patterns without speaking to him. It was like being a somehow invisible participant in a vast but silent play.

He had moments of deep sadness but never cried—maybe the medications he took kept that from happening. Although his memory was less inclusive than it used to be, he remembered what happened between him and Dr. Rohr and that he was now to always be addressed as Father Rohr. On the other hand, Rohr had kept his promise and while his medical assistants, mainly Mr. Harvey, kept giving him drugs, he was never given a memory transplant and so attributed what memory loss he had suffered to the constant medications he had to take. It was also comforting (though he always feared just such a visit) that since the day that he crawled towards Dr. Rohr to service him he hadn't been alone with him once and had only seen him a few times when Rohr occasionally addressed the farm workers on stage from a distance. Of course, virtually all of the workers' incomes were given to The Memory Center.

For not seeing Rohr again he was grateful though he sometimes yearned to see Seven and even that little liar Nadine. Without female contact, it was no wonder that his memory began to shrink. Women begat memories while men were more inclined to exterminate them, he thought.

What memories he did take solace in were chiefly of his childhood when his father seemed to like him more and when he got along better with his mother as well. He would be raking leaves (as he was now) and it would be as if he were raking memories. Not that the dead leaves would bloom again but that they'd seem to come to life in some way, like memory leaves, and he could suddenly remember sledding down the hill in his backyard with his father, as well as a game of catch on the beach with his mother and father smiling in the sunlight.

Rohr had been somewhat benevolent. He'd left him his memory, or most of it, and in the end that was all you could hope for. Sometimes, of course, he would get nervous when he couldn't remember a name or a place he once knew well. It was like a sudden rearing up of his claustrophobia—or like being an animal with the frantic desire to be human again. Seven had actually given him some good advice about these memory attacks the last time he'd seen her a few weeks or possibly months ago.

"Don't try to remember the thing you can't. Let it go and focus on what you can remember. Later it may come back to you, but if it doesn't, it won't matter. You only have what you remember," she'd said "and what you don't have can't touch you 'cause it doesn't exist."

How he missed Seven! He felt a tear escape his eye and let it roll down his face. Every day he remembered the one time he took Identity and made love with her—how he wished she wasn't on Oblivion and could remember it, too.

"What's the matter? You got the blues today?"

It was Hector, a malcontent and potential troublemaker who was raking leaves next to him now, or pretending to.

"We're never gonna get out of here, you know? We're gonna rot here like babies in the desert unless we do something, don't you know that? Rohr's gonna let us rot. Perform a few more experiments on us for the military and then turn us into rotting zombies."

"The military?" Foster said, sarcastically, but who knew, Hector might be right.

"Yeah, who else do you think funds Rohr? Our government, our military—just two heads of the same beast."

Once again he was being tempted by someone who sounded so definite in their convictions, just as Nadine had.

"I'm sorry. I don't agree with you."

"What? You think washing dishes and picking up horseshit is all you can ask for out of life? I know you. I've looked into you. I know you're still a bright guy."

He kept his head down looking at his pile of leaves. Why did so many people suddenly need to look into each other as if people were mirrors?

"You know what?" Hector said. He had a long scar on the left side of his face that Foster had never asked him about. Though he tried not to, Foster couldn't help staring at it especially since it seemed to be in the shape of an "r."

"You know what?" Hector repeated, "I think you do believe me. You're too intelligent not to. You just don't trust me. They got to you early and often, didn't they?"

Keep your head down, Foster said to himself, keep your head down, it's a trick, just another spy.

"Look, I won't let Rohr keep me on his farm my whole life. I'd rather have the operation than that. He doesn't have the right. You know what I'm saying is true. That's why you won't look at me."

He stared at a single gold and green leaf not remembering what tree it came from. Then he started to panic, feeling the claustrophobia again.

"Look, I've been studying this place like I told you. I've been here since the beginning. I've been here for years, since the beginning of time, ha ha, and I have a plan. I know how to get our of here, but I need your help. I can't do it alone."

Foster looked up from the exotic leaf, saw the scar, then all of Hector's face, then the scar again. "Why me?"

"Are you kidding? Have you seen the 'people' here? They're all zombies. Rohr plucked all their brains out. He wants their memory genes to graft onto his own. He wants to own everyone's memories."

Keep your head down, Rohr is testing you again.

"I'm sorry. I'm not interested. I trust Dr. Rohr."

Hector looked at him as if he were another mirror then he turned and step by step began to retreat from him across the unplowed fields. Hector the human scarecrow.

. . . A week later Foster was transferred from the farm to a much more urban environment near The Memory Center headquarters where he'd last seen Dr. Rohr. (As Foster half suspected, he never saw Hector again.) His type of work was also upgraded, and he was now an assistant editor of New Horizons, The Memory Center newsletter. Foster felt vindicated. He'd been right to resist Hector's offer. Rohr had tested him, and he'd obviously passed the test although Hector, a first-rate actor in Foster's estimation, had been very convincing.

It gave Foster confidence in himself, allowed him to relax a little for the first time in weeks, and as if to reward him, his memory had been returning this last week at a faster clip allowing him to decrease his dosage of the new compound he'd been taking that sometimes played havoc with his bowels. He even got to see Seven once on the street, though she stared blankly at him when he waved at her. Disappointing, of course, but because she was still taking Oblivion, understandable—as Seven herself had predicted.

All things considered, it was a more than satisfactory week. Perhaps, most important of all, he felt he was understanding, if not Dr. Rohr, himself, at least his modus operandi. Still, when he was suddenly summoned to Rohr's office and driven there by a limo, he was shocked and quite nervous. He hadn't even had time to change into his best clothes and barely had time to electro brush his teeth or take a high-speed shower before finding himself standing before Dr. Rohr who was wearing his dark glasses again and sitting at his throne-like chair behind his desk. The high, white walls had paintings on them, but Foster saw only vague splashes of color and was unable to concentrate enough to see what the paintings were depicting.

"Sit down, Greg." Rohr said, gesturing with his right hand, "There's nothing to be alarmed about. On the contrary, I've been getting very good reports about you. You're making excellent progress in every way, and that pleases me and the staff at the Center very much."

"Thank you, Father Rohr."

Dr. Rohr smiled at him for a second, and Foster saw an image of a white cap in the ocean again. "No, I actually called you in to talk to you, if I may, a bit about myself. Does that surprise you?"

"A little."

"It shouldn't. I've always had a lot of respect for your opinion on things, including things that are happening to me, decisions that I have to make. You look puzzled. Let me say it this way. I'm getting older and am realizing that I won't always be able to do the things I've been used to doing. And so decisions, life decisions, have to be made. And, in fact, I've made them. Since one of them involves you, I decided to summon you."

Foster looked at him closely. Was this another trick or test? He had to be as careful as possible and to redouble his attention.

"Here's the problem. I find that in reality there is very little in this world I can decide."

"What do you mean, Dr. Rohr?" Foster said, kicking himself for not calling him "Father Rohr," but Rohr hadn't seemed to notice.

"I mean that Time has already decided almost everything for me. Time is my judge, jury and eventual executioner."

Foster nodded to show his support.

"You don't understand, do you? A couple of days ago I was doing a memory transplant and my hand started shaking so much I could barely finish the operation. Do you see now? Every part of my body is beginning to betray me. I don't even know if I can operate again. What do you

have to say to that?" he said, accusatorily, as if
Foster had committed a crime by simply being
relatively young. "Is it right that this should be
happening to a man like me?"

There was a look of terrible anguish
in Rohr's face now, and Foster suddenly felt
himself strangely moved.

"No, it's not. But even if you can't do any
more operations, you still have The Memory
Center to run."

"Yes...The Memory Center," Rohr said, as
if he could barely recall it, though they were
sitting in one of its many offices. "I've devoted
my life to improving the quality of people's
memories, including my own, but now I find
that memories aren't enough for me."

"But you've helped so many people."

"I was unable to save myself," Rohr said,
"and Charity begins at home, wouldn't you say?
No, Greg, lately I've found that memories, even
the strongest memories I created, even Memo
induced memories, aren't enough for me. Even
taking you, the way I did the last time I saw
you, wasn't what I thought it would be, though
I expected it in advance to be strong enough to
become a vital memory. And it was no different
with Seven or Nadine. I've already all but
forgotten them now. Is that right, that this should
be happening to me?"

"But your discoveries, your work lives on at
the Center."

Rohr smiled ironically. "Do you really
think a bunch of buildings with your name on
them makes up for the extreme insult of one's
imminent death?"

"The buildings are one thing but your ideas
or insights will last forever, Father Rohr," Foster
said, still shaking with emotion.

"My insights were all based on my extreme

cynicism about humanity, the fear of their memories and yet their inability to give them up. Above all, their lack of self discipline and so their need for a surgical solution...look at you... you really are like a little boy, but I'm not your father. Your father wouldn't have thrust himself into your mouth as I did, would he? I'm a terrible sinner, but I can't give up my sins, can I? Don't look at me with tears in your eyes. You remind me of Seven and Nadine. You all remind me of each other. Go find your real father, instead. I'm already too many peoples' father."

"My father is dead, Dr. Rohr."

"I meant in your memory. Find him there; you can handle it. Go find him. I'll inform the guards to let you go. Leave the Center. That's right. You're free to go. That's what I summoned you to tell you. You remind me of too many things. Go," said Rohr, pointing with a shaking but impassioned hand that had already taken off his dark glasses. "Go, little boy, go."

He'd been walking in shadows, in sunset, in darkness. Past the winding, snake-like streets and the dinosaur-like buildings. Dr. Rohr's words still roared in his head. There was no Seven, no Nadine, no one, and it was dark. He'd had two fathers and now he had none. One father had told him to leave and find the first father. His first father had died but was remembered like a figure alone at the top of a tower—perhaps a lighthouse, perhaps just a tower.

My father who art in a tower he repeated over and over as he headed toward what he hoped would be a road where he might hitch a ride, though nobody had done that anymore, except as a joke, for 50 years. At the same time as he hoped for a ride, he continued, in spite of himself, to look for a tower. He was looking for it but at the same time was afraid that at the tower's top he'd find a scarecrow instead of his father, a scarecrow or else Dr. Rohr.

My Father who art a scarecrow in a
—tower who has deserted me, who is
—somewhere in my memory, which has
—deserted me, hallowed be thy name.

He tried to laugh at his improvised words but found that he was dizzy instead. He stopped and sat on a rock that came up to his knees, realizing, as he noticed the trees around him, that he was in the country. He sat on the rock and remembered as much of his father as he could. After that, his mother and himself. He remembered much more than he thought he would until finally the words of Rohr no longer filled his head, the dark no longer appalled him. Then he fell asleep on the rock.

In the morning with the first orange streaks of light he set off again for what he eventually hoped would be his home.